THE RESORT

NICOLE SAINT

THE RESORT

Edited by Chereese Graves

www.nicolesaint.com

Give feedback on the book at: info@nicolesaint.com

facebook.com/nicolesaintauthor

First Edition

Printed in the U.S.A

THE RESORT

When Bea Wheeler walks in on her husband Johnny in bed with her best friend, it's fair to say she's shocked. But when he drops dead at the feet of his wife and mistress, it's the beginning of an eventful year in the life of this socialite. Bea's daughters are suffering through trouble of their own, and when all is said is done, end up moving back home. Is it the Wheeler curse? Is it something Bea did that makes it impossible for herself and her daughters to find a significant other?

And then of course there's the resort, the family business Johnny was running—badly, it now seems, since the resort is on the verge of going under. And so the Wheeler women decide to join forces and perform a small miracle by turning the resort around—and in the process turn their own lives around as well.

CHAPTER 1

Bea was supposed to be at the flower show that afternoon, for which she was one of the organizers. But because of some last-minute hullabaloo with Nancy Parker, who was on the organizing committee, and insisted all committee members wear some shade of pink—in line with the flower of the year: the pink rose—she had returned home to change. Apparently Nancy didn't approve of the caramel-colored blouse she was wearing, nor of her skirt, which she deemed too short and inappropriate for a flower show, fearing it might detract from the exhibition's main feature: the flowers. Also, Nancy's husband had a wandering eye, and had recently told his wife that 'The Wheeler woman's got great legs.'

And so it was that Bea walked into the house she shared with her husband of forty years, hurried up the stairs, uttering silent curses about Nancy Parker's outrageous vestimentary edicts, and swept into the bedroom to change.

At first she didn't know what she saw. A pair of hairy buttocks in her bed that could only belong to her husband Johnny, a combination of male grunting sounds and a woman's ecstatic screams, and then her own sharp intake of breath. Poking its way past the hairy buttocks, a blond head became visible, and when Bea realized the head belonged to her best friend Juda Andrews, she actually thought her heart stopped beating for a moment, even as her throat seized up.

Alarmed by his partner's sudden lack of responsiveness, Johnny now also turned to look over his shoulder, and when he caught sight of his wife, standing there like a frozen statue, he spoke the famous words: "It's not what it looks like."

What it looked like was that Johnny was enjoying carnal relations with Bea's best friend in their marital bed, under the roof they'd shared for over four decades. And so once she'd recovered from the shock, and had ascertained that her heart had not actually stopped beating, nor her lungs pumping, she somehow made it to the walk-in closet located on the other side of the bedroom, and started rifling through the rack, in search of a pink blouse and accompanying pink skirt.

And even though she realized the utter irrationality of her behavior, she couldn't stop herself. From the next room, furious whisperings reached her ear, her husband and his mistress engaging in an impromptu attempt at damage control. Bea's hands were shaking as she rifled through her assortment of clothes, though her mind was oddly calm and poised. All she could think of was to get out of there as soon as possible, though to do so she would have to face the adulterous duo again, which she simply refused to do.

"Bea?" a voice came from the bedroom. It was Johnny, and his honeyed tones told her he was employing the same voice he had once used on their daughters when they were being unreasonable. In other words: if they didn't fall in line with their father's dictums. "Can you come out of there, honey? We need to talk about this."

"Yes, Bea," Juda piped up, her voice a little quivery. "I would like to explain."

A sudden rage took hold of her and she stomped out of the closet and into the bedroom, for some reason clutching a peignoir in her hand, and said, "No need to explain. I think it's pretty obvious what's going on here."

Both Johnny and Juda were dressed, with Johnny eyeing her closely, as if she were a bomb that could go off at any moment. His face was flushed, she now saw, his brow wet with sweat, and the few wisps of gray hair he still possessed plastered to his skull. For a man usually determined to engage in as little physical exercise as humanly possible, he'd probably used up all the energy he possessed to partake in these illicit intimacies.

"How long has this been going on?" she demanded, throwing down the peignoir and folding her arms across her chest.

Johnny exchanged a guilty look with Juda. "Well..." he said.

"That long, huh?" said Bea. She directed a withering look at her best friend—soon to be her ex-best friend. "And you..." she began, but then words failed her.

"I'm sorry, Bea," said Juda, and there was some hand-wringing going on, accompanied by guilty glances in her direction. "We never meant for—"

"For me to find out? No, I'm sure you didn't," Bea snapped. She put a hand to her cheek, and discovered that her hand was ice cold. Either that, or her face was as hot and flushed as Johnny's.

"It just happened," said Johnny, gesturing helplessly in the general direction of the bed. Almost as if trying to convey the notion that the whole thing was an anomaly. That whatever was going on here had happened outside of his own will.

Like an earthquake, maybe, or a tornado. In other words, some natural disaster.

"I need to get back," said Bea, who was starting to feel a little nauseous.

"Bea!" said Johnny, taking a step in her direction.

And as he did, suddenly his face contorted into a sort of painful grimace, then he was clutching at his chest, and before she knew what was happening, he collapsed to the floor at her feet.

"Johnny!" Juda cried as she rushed to his side.

The whole scene played out in front of Bea, almost as if she wasn't a part of it. As if it was happening to other people, with her far removed from the room.

"Call an ambulance!" Juda said. And when Bea still didn't make a move, frozen as she was to the spot where she stood, Johnny's mistress rushed to the bed, grabbed her phone from the nightstand—Bea's nightstand—and dialed 911.

And all the while the only thing Bea could think was that now she wasn't going to be able to get to the damn flower show—and how upset Nancy Parker would be.

CHAPTER 2

Lauren glanced around the restaurant. It was filled to capacity as usual. Their favorite eatery for many years, The Franklin in Brooklyn had long enjoyed the custom of her and her husband Jack. In fact they'd been coming here for so long they were on a first-name basis with owner Mikhail and his lovely wife Susanna, who offered the most delicious Greek food in all of Brooklyn, and at a reasonable price, too.

"This is just lovely," she said as she gave her husband a grateful look across the table. "How did you manage to squeeze us in on such short notice?" The place was usually packed for Sunday lunch.

"Remember Mikhail once told us he always had a place for his favorite customers? Well, I decided to take him up on that." Jack returned her smile, and placed a hand on top of hers, the warmth pleasantly seeping into her fingers.

"Such a wonderful surprise," she said. It had been months since they'd gone out on a date like this. Sundays mostly consisted of Kimmy and Kitty joining them for dinner at home. But the twins were enjoying their spring break in

Florida, so it had looked like it would be just the two of them that day. Which had saddened her to some degree. Having grown up with two sisters, in a house that was always filled with life, she still wasn't used to their girls having struck out on their own, leaving their parents alone in a home that frankly was way too big for them now. So when Jack told her he had a treat planned for them, she was overjoyed.

"I have some news for you," said Jack, and for the first time she noticed that he looked a little furtive.

A tiny frown marred her brow as she asked, "News? What news?"

A brief smile flickered across his face, then he leaned in and lowered his voice. "I got a tattoo."

She stared at the man she'd been married to for the past twenty years. "A tattoo?"

He nodded, and rolled up the sleeve of his right arm to show her a tattoo on his wrist. It depicted a guitar.

"And then there's this," Jack continued, and showed her something on his phone. It was an email he'd received.

"What's this?" she asked as she took the phone.

"My audition," he said proudly.

"Audition? What audition?"

And as her husband proceeded to explain that he'd signed himself up to audition for a well-known nationally televised talent show, and that he'd been selected for the first round, she couldn't help but wonder if she'd suddenly landed in an episode of the Twilight Zone. Who was this man and what had he done to her husband?

"I want to be a singer," said Jack. "A rock singer."

"You sing?" she asked. She couldn't remember him ever expressing an interest in singing before. He worked as an accountant, not exactly an artistic endeavor.

"I do," he said as he lovingly rubbed his tattoo. "In fact singing has always been my great passion."

"But… you never told me about this."

"I know," he said, a cloud passing over his cheerful face. "By the time we met I'd already given up on my dream, and then when the twins were born, I put the whole idea on the back burner, figuring I might come back to it at some point. And apparently that point is now." He was beaming at her, and she didn't know how to respond. But when he proceeded to explain to her the ins and outs of his talent show adventure, it was clear there was no need for her to respond, since he was doing all the talking, and all she had to do was listen and be amazed by his 'news.'

Turns out he'd been planning the whole thing for months, keeping her in the dark the entire time. He even got this tattoo applied weeks ago, which made her wonder how she hadn't seen it before. It was true, of course, that their love life had taken something of a hit in recent years, especially when Jack's career had taken off, and he'd spent long days at the office—sometimes deep into the night.

But she'd figured that it was just a temporary thing. Something most couples go through. That at some point the passion and the fire would return. And even if they didn't, that their love would evolve into something deeper—more mature.

And now he'd gotten a tattoo and was launching himself as a rock singer?

"This is just a hobby, though, right?" she asked. "You're not quitting your job or anything?" But when he gave her a sort of sad look, her heart sank. "Jack!"

"It takes a lot of time and energy to launch yourself as an artist these days," he said. "And so I was thinking about taking a sabbatical. A year, maybe two. To really make a go at this thing, you know. And I already got some great contacts."

"Contacts? What contacts?"

It was true that their costs and living expenses would

decrease when the twins finished college and found jobs, but still. If they had to live off their savings, they wouldn't last very long. And also, in the economy they were having, quitting a good job like the one he had just wasn't something you did.

"Well, I met this guy online, who's really killing it with his YouTube videos," Jack explained, excitement making his eyes sparkle. "I slid into his DMs one night, and we've struck up a real connection, you know. And he's been encouraging me to take this thing to the next level."

"What thing? What level?" she asked. This fun date was quickly turning into a nightmare.

"My singing," he said, leaning back. "I'm taking my singing online. Really going for it. Giving it everything I've got and really committing myself to my art."

"But…"

His exuberance waned and a hard look came over him. "I knew you wouldn't understand," he said, suddenly sounding and looking like a petulant child.

"Of course I understand. But don't you think we should talk about this first?"

"We are talking about it, Lauren. That's what we're doing right now. We're talking."

"I know, but it seems to me you've already decided what you're going to do."

"In a sense, I guess you could say I have," he admitted. He was staring at his tattoo, then tapped the table and looked up at her, a determined gleam in his eyes. "There's no easy way to say this, so I'm just going to come out and say it."

"Say what?"

"Lauren," he said, and took a deep breath, "I want a divorce."

She was still reeling from the shock of his announcement when her phone chimed. And since it was lying next to her plate, she saw that it was her mom. In a sort of reflex action, she picked up.

"Lauren," her mom's voice came, "it's your dad. He's had a heart attack."

"What?" she cried. "Is he all right?"

"I'm afraid not, honey," said her mom. "He's dead."

CHAPTER 3

Jill was at the airport when the call came. She was waiting to grab her suitcase from the luggage belt when her phone announced that her mom wanted to talk to her. She picked up with a frown on her face. She hated this part of traveling: having to wait for your luggage, with the remote fear that the airline has somehow managed to lose it along the way and ship it to Tahiti or Berlin.

"Yeah, Mom," she said as she pushed her sunglasses up her nose.

"I'm afraid I have some bad news," said her mother.

"What bad news?" she asked.

"It's your dad. He had a heart attack."

"Oh, God. Is he all right?"

"No, he's dead," said Mom.

"Dead? What do you mean, dead?"

"Are you still in India?"

"No, I'm at the airport."

"What airport? The Indian airport?"

"I'm in New York, Mom. What do you mean, dead? How can Dad be dead?"

"Just come home, will you? I already told Lauren, and now I'm calling Grace."

"I don't understand," said Jill as she watched her suitcase sail right past her nose. Too late, she reached out. Lucky for her, a handsome man must have noticed her move, for he plucked the suitcase from the belt with practiced ease, and deposited it at her feet with a charming smile. She gave him a quick smile in return. "How old is Dad? Fifty? Fifty-five?"

"Sixty-two," said her mother.

"Sixty-two is too young to die," she said as she extended the handle on her suitcase and started rolling it in the direction of the exit.

"Well, apparently he didn't know that," said her mom, and Jill was surprised by the note of acerbity in her mother's voice. She wasn't usually this cynical. In fact this whole conversation struck her as particularly surreal, with mom behaving very strangely indeed. Probably the shock, she thought. Much to her surprise, she wasn't feeling the shock herself. Maybe she'd have a delayed response to the news, like you sometimes read about. "So are you coming home or not?"

"I'm coming home," she said, and felt deeply sad as she spoke the words.

She hated going home. Home wasn't home to her as much as a place she'd always been anxious to get away from. Home was the kind of staid, boring life her sisters had chosen. And her parents, of course. And so the moment she had been in the position to flee Hampton Cove, she had, and had been traveling the world ever since. Which had earned her a reputation as a globetrotter.

Though to be fair, she'd mainly stayed in one place these last couple of years. Goa, India, had quickly become her new home, Antoine, the guru who ran the commune which had become her new home having given her not only a new name—Manara—and a new identity, but also a new purpose in life: finding her bliss. Her spiritual self. Enlightenment. It was a hard path, but also a rewarding one, and one that had made this eternal rebel finally decide to settle down.

The fact that her spiritual journey had led to Antoine's bed, with her becoming his girlfriend, hadn't detracted from the seriousness with which she'd approached this new phase in her life.

Her parents had freaked out, her sisters had marveled, and she had flourished, living her best self and knowing she'd finally found her true purpose in life.

Until last week, when Antoine had chosen one of the other girls he was involved with to accompany him on a trip to Europe. It was only when they'd left that it was discovered that he had also taken a large sum of money along with him. In fact all the money the commune had collected during the season, when the commune was at its busiest, with many visitors filling Antoine's coffers.

Now those coffers were empty, and the Indian authorities had seized all remaining assets, and were conducting a full investigation into the commune's business affairs, after reports of financial malfeasance had reached their ears.

Turns out Antoine was nothing but a common thief, who'd defrauded not only his followers, but also the government and a host of local businesses. According to the latest news he'd flown himself and his favorite girlfriend to Barbados, where he'd boarded the private yacht he'd bought himself and was now sailing the seven seas, and probably having a big laugh at the fools who'd ever believed in him.

And so for the first time in five years, Jill Wheeler was home again—back to the place she had escaped.

As she stood waiting at the taxi stand, the same handsome

stranger who'd been so helpful with her luggage, strode up to her, offering her a dazzling smile. "Heading into town?" he said. And when she nodded, "Want to share a cab?"

Under different circumstances she would have said yes, but after being so unceremoniously dumped by Antoine, and her mom's terrible news, the last thing she needed was to share a cab with a handsome stranger, so she politely declined.

Somehow she didn't believe that her dad was dead. Her mom had sounded so weird on the phone that she just figured she was mistaken. Maybe she just thought he had died, but in actual fact he was simply laid up in hospital. Yeah, that was probably it. Dad had a heart attack, and the doctors were working on him.

They'd save him, of course. Dad was too young to die. Men his age didn't die.

Men like Dad didn't die, period. They just didn't. They lived forever.

CHAPTER 4

Bea patiently waited for her oldest daughter to pick up. She wondered now why she was phoning Grace last. Was it because she was afraid of Grace's response? Mother and daughter hadn't always seen eye to eye, and had often clashed when the girls were growing up. Even in recent years a certain frostiness had persisted between the two women, even though she'd gone out of her way to make Grace feel as welcome in her childhood home as her two sisters.

Somehow, though, her eldest had insisted on keeping her distance, both emotionally but also physically, by moving as far away from home as she could. For the past seven years she'd lived and worked in San Francisco, only returning home for the holidays, and even then she'd missed quite a few of them. Too busy at the high-powered job she had working for Jay Polys, the enigmatic CEO of the eponymously named Polys, the popular ride-sharing company based out west.

Rumor had it—at least according to Lauren—that Grace

was having an affair with her CEO. If she was, she'd never bothered to tell her mom or dad about it.

Finally, Grace picked up. "Yes, Mom," she said in her customary clipped tones. Bea could tell that her daughter was busy, busy, busy again, as usual, and would cut her off in under a minute, the way she always did.

"I'm afraid I've got some bad news, honey," she began.

"Can this wait?" said Grace with the same breathless curtness. "I'm really in the middle of something here."

"It's your dad," she said.

"Look, I'll have to call you back," Grace said, and Bea thought she sounded even more harried and distracted than usual.

"Is everything all right?" she asked.

"Later, Mom," said Grace, and abruptly disconnected.

Bea frowned at her phone. For a moment she thought about sending a text. But she quickly dismissed the thought. She could hardly break the news of Grace's dad's passing by text. Still, she needed to be told. Grace had always been Johnny's favorite. His death would be a big blow to her. As it was to her, of course. Though coming upon the shocking news that Johnny had actually been cheating on her with her best friend, his death almost seemed like an afterthought. Or as if it hadn't actually happened. In fact when the paramedics had been working on him, it had all seemed so unreal. Like a movie playing out in front of her—not reality.

Juda had seemed more upset than her. Crying and wailing and generally being completely shocked by what was happening. She was also the one who'd jumped into the ambulance, with Bea driving behind them in her own car. And she'd been the one who broke down when the doctor told them that Johnny hadn't made it. That he had died on the way to the hospital, which she had already surmised by the fact that they'd turned off the siren and had slowed down their speed.

Still, it wasn't Juda who'd organize the funeral, was it? Or deal with the aftermath of Johnny's death. She now wondered if she had to invite her husband's mistress to the funeral. Was there some kind of protocol that handled such a contingency? She would have to discuss it with the funeral director. And the girls, of course.

Oh, dear Lord. How was she going to break the news to the girls about how their beloved dad had died? Now that was another tough one.

Twenty minutes later, when Grace still hadn't returned her call, and wasn't picking up her phone, she decided to leave a message. "Grace, honey, your dad had a heart attack this afternoon. Please call me as soon as you hear this." She wavered, wondering whether to add that Johnny was dead, but then decided against it. The same way you don't announce a girl's father's sudden death by text, you don't blurt it out on their voicemail either.

So she disconnected, and hoped Grace wouldn't be too busy to return her call.

* * *

Grace stared daggers at the HR woman who was reading her the riot act. And all because she had dared to protest the conditions of her termination.

"Look, I don't know what you've heard, but this ethics complaint is complete bullshit," she said the moment she managed to get a word in edgewise.

"I'm sorry, Grace," said the woman. "But this comes from Polys himself."

"Of course it does," she said, trying to control herself.

"I think he's being very generous, considering your behavior."

The HR director gave her a censorious look, the same look Grace had already received from several of her colleagues, once the news had got out that she was being let go.

It was all so unfair. But then what did she expect? When you're caught having an affair with the big boss, and he files an ethics complaint against you, claiming you were trying to seduce him, and he's the innocent victim, it's your word against his. And since at Polys everything revolved around Jay Polys, she never stood a chance.

"Your severance package," said the HR director, and started rattling off the terms of the deal Polys had put in place to get rid of her. To be fair, it wasn't a bad deal. He could have simply chucked her out. Then again, her reputation was in tatters, and it was obvious she'd never work at the same level at another company again. No boss would hire her now—unless he was a sick pervert, of course.

And since she was done fighting and being angry, in the end she signed on the dotted line, grabbed her box and her potted plant, and slunk off—an ignoble end to an illustrious career.

She was riding the elevator down when she remembered her mother's call. She took her phone out of her pocket and listened to the voicemail Mom had left. And as the truth of her mother's words sunk in, she closed her eyes and leaned against the mirror, the glass cool against her burning forehead.

Just when you think things can't get any worse, that's when they do.

She looked up when the elevator passed the floor she'd spent the better part of the past seven years on. She could even see her former office through the elevator's glass doors, a fact she'd always felt oddly proud of for some reason.

Now all she saw was that her former boss—and former lover—was giving a farewell speech to the collected workforce.

Polys had been sold to a Chinese investor, making Jay Polys a billionaire, and obviously very happy about this achievement, as he stood toasting the takeover with a glass of champagne in his hand.

It was probably the main reason he had decided to turn on her when their relationship had become public knowledge. In light of the takeover, he couldn't risk tarnishing his reputation, so he decided to throw her under the bus instead.

As the elevator slowly slid down, Jay's eyes briefly met hers. But then he quickly turned away again. Just like his company, she was ancient history.

CHAPTER 5

Johnny Wheeler's body was still in the hospital morgue, which was where Bea Wheeler was glancing at him now, accompanied by her three daughters.

"When are they going to move him to the funeral parlor?" asked Lauren. She'd been pressing a tissue to her nose and her eyes were red-rimmed from crying.

"I'm not sure," said Bea. "I'd have to ask the funeral director."

"I don't believe this," said Grace, who'd flown in overnight. "I mean, how could this happen?"

She would have explained in great detail how this had happened, but now didn't seem like the right time.

"He was still so young," said Jill.

"He was sixty-two," Bea pointed out.

"Which is still very young," Jill insisted.

"I know, right?" said Grace. "Sixty-two is too young to die." She frowned at her mom. "You still haven't told us what happened exactly, Mom."

"Not here," said Bea. Not now.

Her three girls were quiet for a moment, saying a silent prayer to their dad, who had died too young, then they left the viewing room. A chaplain stood at attention, in case they needed pastoral support, but none of them had taken him up on his offer. They were going to have to come to terms with this in their own way and in their own time.

Once they'd all returned to the house, they naturally flocked to the big kitchen. And as Lauren, Jill and Grace took a seat at the kitchen counter, Bea watched them and thought: just like old times. In fact she couldn't remember the last time they'd all sat like this. Must have been years ago.

"So what's going to happen now?" asked Lauren.

"Now we have to arrange the funeral," said Bea.

She was still not feeling like herself, as if she was drifting somewhere high above, looking down on the world—like a visitor to her own life.

"Can I stay here for a while?" asked Lauren, causing the others to look up in surprise.

"Of course you can stay here," said Bea.

"What about Jack?" asked Jill. "Is he also coming over?"

Lauren took a deep breath. "Jack wants to file for divorce." When the others all gasped in shock, she added, "He wants to become a rock star."

"What are you talking about?" said Grace, who didn't look amused.

"It's true," Lauren assured them. "He took me to our favorite restaurant, and announced that he wants to become a rock star. He also wants a divorce. He feels that he's been suppressing his dream of being a singer, and now that the twins are out of the house, the time has come for him to finally live that dream."

"I didn't even know that Jack could sing," said Jill.

"Neither did I," Lauren assured her. "And to be honest, I don't think he can."

"I get that he wants to live his dream," said Grace, "but why the divorce?"

Lauren shrugged. "He feels that I've been holding him back all these years. Pushing him to become a corporate rat, and staying in a job that he hates."

"I was also dumped," Jill now announced. "By my guru, who turns out to be a cheat and a fraud."

"Oh, Jill," said Bea, feeling for her girls. What was happening? Was the whole world falling apart all of a sudden?

"Yeah, he sailed off into the sunset with another girl, and left us to pick up the pieces. So I decided to bail, and here I am." She spread her arms. "The family's big failure has done it again."

"You're not the family's biggest failure," said Grace. "That would be me." When all eyes turned to her, she added, "I've been fired from my dream job."

"You were fired!" Bea cried. "But, honey, why?"

Grace shrugged. "Polys was sold to an investment company, and they're going through the personnel files, reorganizing and restructuring."

"But you love your job!" said Lauren. "You love that job so much!"

"Yeah, I did. But clearly the job didn't love me. So could I have my old room back, Mom? Looks like I don't have a place to stay anymore."

"Oh, sweetie, of course," said Bea. "You don't even have to ask."

"Can I also have my old room back?" asked Jill.

Lauren smiled. "Just look at us. Three losers."

"You're not losers," said Bea. "None of you." In fact if anyone was the biggest loser, it would be her.

"Okay, so now that we've established that we're all lousy at keeping relationships," said Lauren, "or hanging on to our jobs," she added, with a pointed look at Grace, who rolled her eyes, "can you finally tell us what happened to Dad, Mom?"

Bea nodded. And as she told the story of what happened the day before when she walked in on Johnny and Juda, she could tell from her daughters' faces that they were as shocked as she was about their dad's betrayal. A betrayal that had probably led to his death. Though according to the hospital, Johnny's heart attack was an accident waiting to happen.

"I don't believe this," said Lauren. "Dad and Aunt Juda?"

"How long had this been going on?" asked Grace with a frown.

"I have no idea," said Bea. "You'd have to ask Juda."

"Oh, I will," Grace assured them. "In fact I might go over there now."

"Please don't," said Bea. "It's only going to create more trouble."

"I wonder if Uncle Jim knows," said Lauren.

"I doubt it," said Bea quietly. Juda and her husband Jim had been their closest friends for over forty years. They'd spent holidays together, vacationed together, gone skiing together. The girls called them Uncle Jim and Aunt Juda, even though they weren't related. She'd always considered Juda her best friend, and Jim had been Johnny's friend going back even further, from before they were married.

And now this. If Jim found out, he'd be devastated, Bea knew. Just like she was.

For the rest of the evening they talked about the events that were probably going to shape their lives for the foreseeable future, and as she warmed up some meatballs and spaghetti sauce from the freezer, and they sat down for an impromptu dinner, Bea couldn't help but look at her three girls and feel a certain satisfaction—in spite of the terrible tragedy that had brought them all together.

It warmed her mother's heart to have her daughters under the same roof again—even if it was only for a couple of days. There was no doubt in her mind that once the funeral was over, Jill would fly off to India or Thailand or Nepal again, to pursue her spiritual journey. Lauren would return to Brooklyn to deal with the aftermath of her divorce. And Grace might have been edged out of the job she loved so much, but she was tough and ambitious, and would soon be pursuing other opportunities that would put her back on top of the corporate ladder.

Just such a pity that none of them had any luck in love. Like Bea herself, they were all single again. Jill had been dumped by some crook guru, Lauren's husband was divorcing her, and Grace... Well, Grace was too busy making a career to have a family, which was just as sad as what was happening with her sisters, of course.

After dinner, the girls helped their mother clean up, and then it was time to go to bed. Bea had turned their bedrooms into guest rooms, which was just as well, since they were going to need them for the next couple of days. The only room that wasn't available anymore was Grace's, actually. Johnny had turned it into a home gym at some point, though he'd never actually gotten round to using it.

"Too bad Dad didn't spend a little more time in here," said Grace as she stared at her old room, which was now full of shiny fitness equipment. "If he had, he would still be alive."

"You don't know that," said Jill. "Dad could have been suffering from some congenital heart disease. A malfunctioning heart valve or something."

"We'll figure it out tomorrow," Grace assured her sister. "When we talk to the doctor. And Juda," she added, shooting her mom a warning glance not to interfere in this fact-finding mission she had planned for herself. She was going to get to the bottom of this affair business or die trying, that much was obvious. "So that leaves one big question," Bea's eldest said. "Where am I going to sleep tonight?"

"You can bunk with me," Lauren offered magnanimously. "I've got the biggest bed."

Which was true, as her room contained a double bed, put there for when she and Jack would spend the night at the house over the holidays.

"Great," Grace muttered. "But don't even dream of putting those cold feet of yours against mine in the middle of the night. If you do I promise I'll scream."

"I don't have cold feet."

"Yes, you do."

"I do not!"

"Girls, girls," said Bea. "Please don't fight." She then lowered her voice and whispered to Lauren, "I'll prepare you a hot water bottle. How does that sound?"

"Sounds great, Mom," Lauren whispered back.

Yep. Just like old times.

CHAPTER 6

Mom had taken a sleeping pill and had gone to bed, and since none of the girls felt even remotely tired, all three of them ended up in the verandah, discussing recent events. Shocking as the circumstances were, Grace was glad to see her sisters. She wouldn't have admitted it to anyone, but it was true. Living out west and focused on her career as she had been for the past couple of years, she'd missed hanging out with Jill and Lauren. It was just sad that it took Dad dying for the three of them to come together again—even if it was only for a short time.

"I still can't believe about Dad and Aunt Juda," said Jill. "I mean, who would have thought?"

"I think we should probably stop calling her that," said Lauren.

"Calling her what?"

"Aunt Juda."

"I doubt we'll be seeing much of her and Uncle Jim now," said Grace as she took a sip from her glass of wine. She was feeling slightly tipsy, though it could have been an effect of the flight, of course. Combined with being fired from her job, Dad dying, and knowing that he'd been cheating on Mom for who knows how long. "If they've got any dignity they won't come to the funeral."

"Oh, I'm sure they will come to the funeral," said Lauren. "Dad was Jim's best friend."

"I'm not so sure he still feels that way," said Jill. "After what happened."

"And how do you know he knows?" said Grace. "Juda won't have told him about the affair, and if Mom didn't tell him either he's not going to know."

"This is Hampton Cove, hon," said Lauren. "Everybody knows everything about everyone."

"Which makes it hard to believe this affair could go on for however many years without anyone knowing about it," said Jill. "I mean, someone could have told Mom. Or Uncle Jim."

"I wonder how long the affair was going on, exactly," Grace mused. "Do you think they were seeing each other already when we were little? Or was this a recent thing? Inquiring minds want to know."

"Frankly I don't care," said Jill. "And besides, it's ancient history now anyway. Dad is gone, and he's not coming back."

"I think there must be some kind of curse on this family," said Lauren as she sank a little deeper into the wicker chair she'd claimed for herself. "First Dad cheats on Mom with her best friend, then your guru runs off with some other woman," she said with a nod to Jill, "and it wouldn't surprise me if Jack wasn't secretly involved with someone, too. I mean, I just can't believe he would divorce me just because he wants to become a singer. That just sounds too ridiculous."

"So how about you, Grace?" asked Jill.

"What about me?" said Grace, moodily staring into the darkness of the backyard.

"How is your love life going? As disastrous as ours? Worse? Better?"

She clamped her lips together for a moment, wondering whether to tell them or not. But finally decided there was no point in keeping secrets. "Yeah, I'm a victim of the Wheeler curse, too," she admitted. When her sisters gawked at her, she added, "I was having an affair with my boss."

"Wait, what?" said Lauren, trying to sit up straighter and failing miserably. These wicker chairs were pretty unforgiving that way.

"Not Polys!" said Jill, perking up to a considerable extent.

"Yes, Polys," she said. "Only when his secretary walked in on us one morning when we were feeling particularly frisky, he couldn't get rid of me fast enough." As she related the story, she experienced the same keen sensation of betrayal all over again. How Polys had told her it was over, and had gone behind her back to file an ethics complaint against her—claiming she had tried to seduce him and he had found it impossible to say no, since she held such a powerful position in the company.

"Bullshit," said Jill, as she stared at her sister with incredulity written all over her face.

"No, that's what happened," said Grace.

"He actually fired you for having an affair with him? The man is evil!"

"Yeah, good riddance," said Lauren. "Though too bad about your job, of course."

"And the guy," said Grace quietly. Even though Jay had behaved abominably, she couldn't deny that she still had feelings for the guy. Before the affair had exploded in their faces, things between them had been going great, actually. He'd told her that his marriage was on the rocks, and that it was only a matter of time before he would get a divorce and make things official between them.

"So why did he dump you, exactly?" asked Lauren. The wine was making her a little sluggish, and her speech a little slurred.

"Some big investor was in the process of buying Polys. They've been negotiating the deal for months, and Jay couldn't risk any bad exposure, since the investor is very sensitive about traditional family values."

"So if your affair leaked, he might renege on the deal," Lauren said, nodding.

"Unless Polys could prove that he was squeaky clean, and I was the bad one. The instigator, with him as my helpless victim. So he got rid of me, kicked me out of the company, and last I heard the deal went through and Jay Polys is now officially a billionaire." She raised her glass. "And I'm jobless and homeless." Homeless because she couldn't possibly afford her old apartment anymore.

"You're not homeless, sweetie," said Lauren. "I'm sure Mom would be only too glad to have you live at home again."

"Oh, goodie," Grace muttered darkly. For some reason she simply couldn't escape this place, could she? And since she'd burned her bridges on the West Coast, and possibly everywhere else, she was probably going to be stuck here for the foreseeable future.

"Don't look so sad, sis," said Jill. "I'm also stuck here. In fact it looks like we're all stuck here."

They glanced to Lauren, who nodded in confirmation. "If the divorce goes through, we'll have to sell the apartment. Which means I won't have a place to live. So looks like it's home sweet home for me, too, you guys."

"Oh, God," said Jill, downing her drink in one big gulp.

"What did I tell you?" said Lauren. "It's the Wheeler family curse!"

CHAPTER 7

As it was, they had one more problem to deal with, and a pretty big one at that: the resort.

Johnny Wheeler had been running the Hampton Cove Resort & Spa for years, ever since his father-in-law had retired, and subsequently passed away. And so now that he was gone, too, the question was who would run the resort.

Since Mom was still under the weather after what happened, and had refused to leave the house, or to set foot inside the resort, where she knew people would talk about her husband's affair with his best friend's wife, it was up to the three Wheeler sisters to take matters into their own hands.

For that purpose a meeting had been arranged at the resort with Dad's assistant manager, Michele Bouvier, and with the accountant, Nicolas Holmes. Between the two of them, they knew everything there was to know about the state of the family business, and how best to proceed.

The meeting took place in Dad's office, located in the staff wing of the resort, where most of the administrative staff were housed. Located behind the lobby, it was the heart of the place, and not unfamiliar to the three sisters, since all of them, at some point in the past, had worked there in some capacity, mainly summer and student jobs, but still. All of them were well known to the staff.

"Okay, so first off," said Michele, who was a stately woman in her late fifties with an abundance of red hair and entirely too much makeup, "my sincerest condolences to your family. Johnny's death has come as a great shock to all of us here at the Hampton Cove Resort & Spa."

"Thanks," said Lauren quietly.

Simply the fact of sitting in her dad's office, in his personal space, felt both comforting and unsettling. She kept expecting him to walk in through the door any minute.

"Yes, my sincerest condolences," Nicolas murmured. The accountant was dressed in his usual suit and tie, and looked his customary debonair self.

"The thing is," said Michele, taking control of the meeting, "that I have some bad news of my own to share with you."

Lauren looked up in surprise. "Not… your husband?"

"No, my husband is fine," said Michele. She paused, then nodded to herself, and said, "I'm afraid I'm leaving."

"Leaving? What do you mean?" asked Grace.

"I'm leaving the resort."

"But… you can't leave," Jill blurted out.

"Yes, I can. And I will."

"Oh, boy," said Nicolas, adjusting his tie.

"Look, I didn't want to do this to you—not with your dad dying and all, but this is a decision I made a long time ago. I actually discussed it with your dad several times, and he promised me he was going to find a replacement, so I could train him or her to take over from me. But clearly he was too busy elsewhere to bother, because this has been going on for a year now."

"But..." Jill said, glancing at her two sisters.

"The thing is that your dad was the general manager and I was his assistant. But in actual fact I've been running the resort for the past five years. In fact your dad hardly ever showed his face around here anymore."

"It's true," Nicolas confirmed.

"And when I told him things couldn't go on like this, he kept making me all kinds of promises. At one point he even said he'd step down and make me general manager. He was going to hire an assistant manager so I wouldn't have to do everything on my own. He was going to do all kinds of things. But in the end he did nothing, and frankly I'm fed up."

Sounded like Michele had been fed up for quite some time, Lauren thought. Which she could totally understand, if she had to run the resort in Dad's absence.

"But what was Dad doing if he wasn't coming in to work every day?" asked Jill.

Both Michele and Nicolas exchanged meaningful glances, and it was obvious that Dad had had other things on his mind for the past five years than running the family business.

"Look, I don't want to say a bad word about your father," Michele said. "He was a great person, and I think I can speak for all of us here at the Hampton Cove Resort when I tell you that we thought the world of him. But he lost focus at some point, and simply couldn't be bothered anymore."

"He also created a lot of debt," said Nicolas carefully.

"Debt?" asked Lauren. "The resort is losing money?"

The accountant nodded. "Your father, I'm afraid to say, used the resort as his personal ATM machine. He took a lot of money out of the business."

"He took money? What for?"

"I have no idea. Unfortunately he didn't take me into his confidence. But rumor has it that he had developed a penchant for fast cars." He gave them a hesitant look. "There was also the fact that he had developed a special... relationship with a close friend of the family."

"Juda Andrews," Grace confirmed. "We know all about that, Nicolas."

The accountant looked relieved. One doesn't want to make a social faux-pas by revealing to the family of a recently deceased beloved father that he was having an affair.

"So you're implying Dad spent the resort's money on his girlfriend?" asked Jill.

"One of our staff members saw Johnny in town, checking out a jewelry store," Michele said. "And I once walked in on him and found him leafing through a travel brochure. Luxury travels," she said with a look of significance at the sisters. "Monaco, St Barts, Courchevel—that's in Switzerland," she added for good measure. "I also noticed that he was wearing an expensive watch the last time he dropped by. I couldn't tell you which brand, but it must have cost a small fortune."

"I know for a fact he was thinking about buying a yacht," said Nicolas. "We had a guest staying here a couple of months back, who owned his own yacht. And your dad got very excited, and wanted to know all about it. Kept asking him questions."

"Mom never told us about any of that," said Lauren with a frown.

"He wouldn't have told her," said Grace. "Not if he was spending all of that money on Juda. Buying her expensive jewelry and taking her on luxury trips to Europe."

"I'm afraid with all the money that's been flowing out of the business and into your father's personal account, the resort is not doing so well at the moment," said Nicolas. "And hasn't been doing well for quite some time."

"Five years," Grace murmured. "At least now we know how long this affair has been going on." She fixed the accountant with a serious look. "You said something about Dad building up debt?"

"The money we were making wasn't enough for Johnny," Michele explained. "So he had started borrowing money against the business."

"Oh, God," said Grace. "How much?"

"At some point we were about a million in the hole," said Nicolas.

For a moment they were all silent. And as the reality of the situation became clear to them, anger sputtered to the surface. "Can't we sue Auntie Juda?" Jill suggested. "Take everything Dad gave her back and sell it to cover the debts?"

"I'm afraid it's not that easy," said Nicolas. "As the owner of the resort, your dad had every right to do with that money as he chose. So I'm afraid you won't have a leg to stand on—legally, I mean."

"Unless we can prove that Dad wasn't of sound mind," said Jill. "I mean, isn't that something we could use?"

"I very much doubt it," said Grace, dryly dismissing Jill's suggestion.

"Okay, so I'm very sorry to have to do this to you," said Michele, getting up. "Especially under the circumstances. But I'm afraid I have to leave."

"You're not quitting right now, are you?!" cried Lauren.

"I'm afraid so," said Michele, a stubborn look on her face. "I've been postponing this for months, and I can't postpone any longer. I gave Johnny every chance to deal with this, and he wouldn't, so this is where I say goodbye." She nodded curtly at the three sisters, who sat staring at the stalwart assistant manager in horror, then repeated, "Goodbye," and walked out of the office.

CHAPTER 8

"Okay, so you better give it to us straight, Nicolas," said Grace, taking control of the situation. "Is this place on the verge of drowning in debt or not?"

"Not," said the accountant with visible satisfaction. "In spite of the standoffish position he took in regards to the resort, your dad was well aware of the problems his behavior had caused, and in recent months had been working on a solution."

"What solution?" asked Grace.

"He had brought in an investor," Nicolas explained. "Who was going to make a considerable cash injection into the business, which would go a long way to wiping out that debt, and even to bring about some long-postponed renovations that should give this place a much-needed boost. A new lease on life, your dad called it. In fact I had a meeting with him about this just last week." His face sagged. "Before he... well, before he died."

"So this investor, is he locked in?"

"He's locked in," Nicolas confirmed. "The contracts were signed and the deal will go through."

"Have you met him?" asked Lauren. "Is he going to play an active role in the running of the business?"

"No, absolutely not. Your dad assured me he won't play a role in the day-to-day business of running the resort at all. He's more like a silent investor. In fact I haven't even met him. None of us have. I don't even know who he is. Or she. Or it."

"It could be a consortium," Grace explained to her sisters. "Or a holding company, simply investing in this place as a way of diversifying their portfolio."

"Your dad assured me it's something along those lines," said Nicolas with satisfaction. He rubbed his hands. "Of course now that Michele is gone, and your dad, a new general manager will have to be found."

"We'll have to discuss this with Mom," said Grace, eyeing her sisters uncertainly. This was entirely new terrain for them. None of them had experience in running a resort. She turned to the accountant. "What role did my mother play in the business? I mean, I understood from Michele's explanation that Dad wasn't actively involved these past couple of years, but what about Mom?"

"Your mother didn't concern herself with anything that was connected with the resort," said Nicolas with a touch of sadness. "In fact I can't remember the last time she dropped by for a visit."

"I think the deal they had was that Dad would run the business," said Lauren, "which would leave Mom free to pursue her own interests."

"What interests?" asked Jill.

"Your mother is very active in several local charities and nonprofits and is on many different committees," said Nicolas. "I know for a fact that she's a member of the committee organizing the annual flower show, she's on the board of the Hampton Cove History Museum, the cultural center, the

Spring Market Fest, the new community center, the library, um..."

"Juda's also on those," said Lauren. "In fact Juda is on all of those with Mom."

"I very much doubt Mom will ever join any of those things again," said Jill.

"Well, she should," said Lauren. "It's Juda who should resign, not Mom."

"We can talk about that later at the house," Grace suggested. "I think it's more important that we figure out what to do about this general manager business."

"We don't have to figure that out right now, do we?" asked Jill, making a face. "I mean, we're not businesswomen. We don't know about any of that stuff."

Lauren turned to Grace. "You're a businesswoman. Maybe you know how to handle this mess?"

Grace frowned. "We'll have to put out a job offer—get in touch with local recruiters. But that's going to take time. And since Michele seems adamant that she's leaving today..."

"She signed a contract for a new position last week," Nicolas explained. "She told your dad about this weeks ago, and he promised he was going to hire a replacement, so she could pass on her knowledge and her experience. Make sure the transition could be handled smoothly. But apparently he had other ideas."

"Oh, Dad," Grace groaned. This was all just too much.

Nicolas coughed a deprecating cough. "I hate to be the bearer of bad news," he began.

"Not more bad news!" Jill cried, throwing up her hands in despair. "I don't know how much more I can take!"

"What is it, Nicolas?" asked Lauren.

"Well, our fitness instructor gave notice this morning. And also, and more importantly, the person in charge of customer relations. So that's two more positions that need to be filled, one more urgent than the other."

"Why are they leaving, do you know?" asked Grace, though she had a good idea what the reason could be.

"Employee sentiment has not been positive," said Nicolas, who didn't seem happy in his role of messenger of these bad tidings. "Rumors have been flying around about the new investor, and about financial difficulties, and even though Michele has done a stellar job trying to hold it all together, with her leaving other members of staff have started looking elsewhere as well. In fact the fitness instructor is following her to the new place."

"Where is Michele going?" asked Lauren.

"She's going to be the new general manager at the Argent."

Grace whistled through her teeth. "Talk about a step up."

The Argent Resort was a swanky five-star resort in Southampton, and one of the Hampton Cove Resort's biggest competitors. Or actually *the* big competitor.

"We should have been able to keep her," said Lauren. "Dad should have made her general manager, and then she wouldn't have left."

"I think Michele would have left anyway," said Nicolas. "The Argent made her an offer she couldn't refuse—an offer your dad would never be able to match."

They were all silent as they processed these new developments. But then Grace, never one to buckle under pressure, slapped her dad's desk once. "Okay, looks like we've got work to do here, people. And a new manager to find."

CHAPTER 9

Steven Lesinske watched as the three Wheeler women emerged from the big boss's office, along with Nicolas, and said their goodbyes. Steven had been in charge of the reception desk for the past three years, taking over when his predecessor retired. Back then the resort was humming, with never a lull in the proceedings, and bookings coming in fast and furious. Lately things had slowed down considerably, and it wasn't a rare thing to have occupancy dropping below sixty percent, which was an unhealthy low for them. He was sure that the Argent was doing much better. In fact he knew that for a fact, for his cousin was the receptionist at Southampton's most popular and prestigious beach resort.

He wondered what was going on now that Jill, Grace and Lauren Wheeler had deigned to honor the resort with their presence. Of their mother there hadn't been a trace in years, and their dad had also managed to make himself scarce, even though he had still carried the title of general manager—in name only.

Steven brought a nervous hand to his lips and was about

to start chewing his nails—a habit he desperately tried to break but so far had been unable to—when a deep voice spoke next to him and a bejeweled hand slapped his own hand away.

"Don't," the voice warned. "Nobody likes a receptionist who chews his fingernails."

"Hello, Hazel," he said, his eyes still fixed on the Wheeler sisters. "Looks like something is happening. You wouldn't happen to know what, would you?"

Hazel, who was about a hundred years old and ran the bookings for the resort, shrugged a pair of bony shoulders. "No idea. Nobody ever tells me anything."

That wasn't necessarily true. In fact one could say that Hazel was the hub of the resort, the spider in the web and the one person in whom everyone confided.

"I saw Michele just now. She came to say goodbye. Said she was leaving."

"Yeah, she said goodbye to me, too," said Hazel. "Good riddance, I say."

"Oh, don't be like that. Michele was a good boss."

"That's just because she's the only boss you've ever known. I can tell you from experience that she was a pretty lousy boss. Case in point: she refused to give me a pay raise again."

"You're already earning more than the rest of us combined, Hazel. You can't possibly expect to earn even more. And besides," he quickly added over Hazel's protestations, "it wasn't Michele you should have asked but big man Wheeler himself."

"Yeah, as if he was going to give me a raise. He needed all the money he could get to buy himself another Ferrari, or his girlfriend another trip to Paris."

It was a sad state of affairs that the resort had been the victim of mismanagement for so many years, run by a guy who couldn't keep his pecker in his pants, and was being strung along by a gold digger, and a woman who couldn't care less about her family's heritage, once the crown jewel of beach resorts in the state. He heaved a deep sigh of regret. "I should have accepted that offer to work at the Argent when I had the chance," he now said. "Then I wouldn't be stuck here with no prospects, in a place that's about to go belly-up any day now."

Hazel's wrinkly face morphed into a look of contempt. "Lord rid us of these Wheelers—and the sooner the better, if you ask me."

"Well, nobody is asking you, are they, Hazel, dearest? Or me."

"They should. Between the two of us we'd do a damn sight better job than Johnny Wheeler ever did. Or his stooge Michele."

Steven didn't bother to comment. Rumor had it that Michele had once stolen a man from Hazel, a man she had designs on, and that's when their rivalry had begun, which still persisted to this day. But Michele was gone now, and if the rumors were true, soon the whole resort would be a thing of the past as well.

Oh, well. He could always find a job at some hotel somewhere. He loved the Hampton Cove, though. The location was amazing, of course, with the beach nearby, and the small town of Hampton Cove within walking distance from the resort. It wasn't perhaps one of the fanciest resorts, like the Argent, but it had a homely feel, a family feel—though Johnny had more or less squandered all of that when he decided to cheat on his wife with this Juda Andrews woman, and to direct his attention elsewhere, ignoring his duties to his wife's family's business.

But then wasn't that often the way? That people didn't

appreciate what they had, and in the process ended up losing what made it so great and wonderful?

But before his thoughts could return to his favorite theme, a guest walked into the lobby, and he perked up. Even if the resort was going down, he'd keep adhering to the principles of hospitality his predecessor had pumped into him before retiring and leaving his young charge at the helm: always make them feel at home!

"Yes, sir," he said. "What can I do for you?" And even as he spoke these well-honed words, in the honeyed tones that were his hallmark, he thought he recognized the young man who had wandered in from the street. If he wasn't mistaken —and he rarely was—this was none other than Tim Deutch, the well-known Hollywood thespian and star of many a blockbuster movie.

Well, take that, Argent.

CHAPTER 10

Tim had the impression that the young man at the reception desk had recognized him, and hoped he would be discreet about the presence of such a famous star at the resort. He told himself not to worry, though. Tim's business manager had personally recommended the place to him, telling him he'd been coming here for years with his family, and had always loved the family atmosphere and the great care the owners took in treating their guests like human beings, not numbers.

Even though he'd grown a mustache and changed the color of his hair from its usual brown to a shiny black, he still wasn't sure he wouldn't be recognized. From the way the receptionist's eyes had flicked up to his, then away again, he had the feeling his ruse was failing. He'd have to go the whole hog again: donning a baseball cap and sunglasses whenever he was out in public. Hopefully it would keep the paps away, for once they smelled blood, they wouldn't leave him alone.

He was using his usual pseudonym to check in, of course, signing as Bob Malone, but the receptionist wasn't fooled, judging from the complicit smile he suddenly gave him and the whispered, "I hope you enjoy your stay, Mr. *Malone*."

At least he hadn't asked for his autograph, or told him how much he loved his latest movie. And as he rolled his luggage down the corridor in the direction indicated, he wondered again about the wisdom of this retreat, as advised by the real Bob Malone, who wasn't just his business manager but also a good friend.

Then again, he could certainly use some downtime, as he'd been working pretty much nonstop since he'd hit the big time three years ago with his first blockbuster hit. He'd filmed the sequel back to back with the third installment in the billion-dollar franchise, and already the studio had green-lit a fourth movie, which was going to be filmed next year in Australia.

But the constant attention, and the level of exposure he'd had to sustain, had exhausted him to the point that he'd started wondering if he'd taken the right path. He never wanted to be a global star or a celebrity. All he wanted was to be an actor, and to entertain people with his art. Not the craziness that was now apparently his life.

He put his suitcase on the bed and walked through to the window and opened it. A gentle ocean breeze billowed through the curtain, and as he gazed out across the beach, and the clear blue of the water beyond, he found himself relaxing for the first time since he'd touched down in New York, some of the tension dissipating.

Maybe this would be a good idea after all.

His phone buzzed and as he took it out, he saw that his agent was trying to reach him. Deciding that was the last thing he needed right now, he put his phone on the table and walked into the bathroom for a long, hot shower.

He was officially on vacation now—the world could wait.

***

ONE ROOM OVER, Terry Davis heard the shower being turned on in the adjacent bathroom. He closed his eyes and gave himself up to thought. Lying on the bed with his hands supporting his head, the old man had been racking his brain trying to come up with a solution for the problem that had been vexing him and his wife Heather. Faithful guests of the resort, they'd been coming here for over fifty years. In fact they'd honeymooned here, and liked it so much they'd been coming back every year ever since. Now almost part of the furniture, they knew the place inside and out, the owners and workers more like family to them than actual staff.

Though it now seemed likely this year would be their last.

He opened his eyes when his wife walked out of the bathroom, pressing a cooling little wet towel to her brow. She sat down on the bed next to him, and they held hands for a moment. No words were spoken. When you were married as long as they were, there was no need for words. The message was clear.

Terry had no regrets, though. They'd led a wonderful life. The biggest tragedy that had befallen them was when they'd discovered they couldn't have kids. Heather would have loved to have kids. She'd been dreaming of having at least two: a boy and a girl. But as it transpired, her dream simply wasn't to be. And they'd accepted that and had moved on.

And now this calamity had come into their lives. He still blamed himself. If only he'd been more careful. Everyone said you had to be careful with these investment advisors. But the guy had been recommended by their banker. Bitcoin was the future, the guy had told them. It was going to blow up big time, and they would triple their investment, maybe even quadruple it. The sky was the limit.

He hadn't been all that interested in tripling their savings, but didn't see the point of leaving it in their savings account either, not with the disappointing interest rates they'd seen. He knew next to nothing about the stock market, and this bitcoin sounded like a great investment. People were always talking about it on television, and some important and well-respected celebrities had been touting it as well. So when the opportunity arose, he decided to go all in and invest.

And that's when the news came that the company they'd used for their investment was a scam. A front for a group of swindlers. Their money had never been invested at all. It had simply been used to pay other gullible investors. The guy who was running the scam had been arrested, but the money was gone. All of their savings—the money they'd worked a lifetime to collect—all gone.

He closed his eyes again. The worst part was the guilt. He was the one who'd pulled the trigger. If it had been up to Heather, she probably wouldn't have been so eager to give their hard-earned savings to this scammer. And to think he used to be so careful about money, back when he still owned his own gardening business. How could he have been so foolish now?

The mattress shifted and he saw that was looking at him with concern in her eyes.

"You're not still beating yourself up about this, are you?" she asked.

He nodded wordlessly. How could he not beat himself up about what he'd done. He'd ruined their lives. Fifty years of happiness gone in one fell swoop.

She pressed his hand. "It'll be all right," she told him. "I just know it will."

He wasn't so sure about that. "I wish I had your optimism," he murmured.

"It's not optimism," she said. "It's faith. You should try some of that yourself."

He gave her a weak smile. "We won't even be able to pay the bill anymore, Heather," he confessed. "We should leave and go home before they kick us out."

But her resolve didn't waver. Instead she said, "It's going to be all right, Terry."

There was a knock at the door and a voice called out, "Maintenance," and Terry lifted himself up from the bed with some effort and walked over to the door.

When he found himself looking into the smiling face of Cole Newman, who was in charge of maintenance, he felt his mood lift somewhat. Hard to feel down when Cole was there. His presence was enough to give a dead person a boost.

"So what seems to be the trouble, Terry?" asked Cole as he put his toolbox on the floor and gave the other man a clap on the back.

"One of the taps in the bathroom stopped working," said Terry. And as Cole walked into the bathroom to take a look, he added, "It's the cold water one."

"See if I can get that fixed for you," said Cole with a wink, and went straight to work.

Terry watched the handyman work for a while, the two men chatting amiably, then he closed the door to the bathroom and returned to Heather. They needed to talk this thing through, for however much his wife liked to believe that some miracle might happen and make everything all right, that simply was not the case.

CHAPTER 11

Cole stuck his head under the sink to try and figure out what could be causing the blockage when the bathroom door gently creaked open, and he heard snatches of conversation drifting in from the next room. And what he heard frankly concerned him a great deal. From what he could fathom, Terry and Heather were having some kind of financial difficulties, and were worried that they wouldn't be able to pay their bill and would be found out and kicked out of the resort.

Cole frowned as he stilled his hand and listened. He hated to eavesdrop like this, especially on two people he considered his friends, but this was serious. He could hear it in the inflection of their voices.

Terry and Heather had been coming to the resort for so long they had probably seen it being built back in the day. They'd certainly been coming there a long time before Cole had started working there, and he had been at his job for twenty-four years now, ever since Johnny Wheeler had personally hired him. Back then he'd been dating the man's daughter, which might explain why he got the job in the first place. But it didn't explain why he was still there now. That could only be explained by the fact that he was good at what he did. The best, in fact. And those weren't his words, but the big boss himself who'd told him so on more than one occasion. Of course this was when Johnny was still running the show, before he decided jumping in bed with his wife's best friend was more fun than managing his wife's family's resort.

Cole's affair with Johnny's daughter had long since ended, if he could even call it an affair. More like a summer fling. They'd been seventeen and he'd been in love, though the same couldn't be said for Grace, who had probably forgotten all about him the moment she left for college and had never come back. At least he'd gotten a great job out of it, and an equally great circle of friends: his colleagues.

Though lately the engine had started to sputter on that front. Michele said goodbye to him that morning, telling him to get out as well if he knew what was good for him, and some other colleagues had taken her advice and had also quit.

Not him, though. If it was up to him, he'd be the last man standing at the Hampton Cove Resort & Spa. He loved his job so much he couldn't imagine working anywhere else. He just knew it wouldn't be the same. Not by a mile.

And that was exactly what worried him: what if Michele was right, and with Johnny dead the place about to go belly-up any moment now? Rumor had it that Johnny had been living it up these last couple of years, spending money he shouldn't have so he could lavish expensive gifts on his girlfriend, and enjoying life in the fast lane for a change.

But according to Nicolas a new investor had come on board, and he was going to finance a complete makeover of the place—put them on track for a bright future, on par with the Argent, still the *numero uno* of beach resorts on the coast. If that was the case, he wanted to be there for that exciting new chapter. Then again, these outside investors could be fickle. They might want to go full bore and throw out the old crew and bring in a bunch of new hires, younger and cheaper and more eager to please the new boss.

He carefully closed the bathroom door. He didn't want Terry and Heather to think he was listening in on their private conversation. But what he'd heard worried him. In fact it worried him so much he decided to have a talk with the manager. Only problem was: now that Michele was gone, and with Johnny dead, who was the new manager?

It didn't take him long to fix that tap, and once he had, he made a show of stomping around, letting Terry know he was finishing up.

The door opened, and he let his friend know the sink was as good as new. The old man gave him a grateful look.

"You're worth your weight in gold, Cole," said Terry. "If I've said it once, I've said it a million times. I sure hope they pay you enough, cause they should."

"Can't complain," said Cole, and glanced over to Heather, who was standing by the window, a hand to her face, and looking visibly distraught.

He felt for her. Never having faced money problems himself, he still could understand it was a tough situation to be in.

And as he said goodbye to the couple, he was pondering the best course of action. He couldn't very well let them know he'd overheard their conversation. They'd be mortified if they knew he knew. But he couldn't just let it go, either. Terry and Heather weren't mere guests. They were family. He had to do something. But what?

And as he was wondering how to proceed, he passed the lobby on his way back to his office, when he almost came face to face with... Grace Wheeler!

She and her sisters were accompanied by Nicolas, and it

was clear that the accountant was giving them the grand tour of the place. Seeing as none of the three sisters had set foot in the resort in years, he just as well might, considering they were probably the new owners now that their dad was gone.

He cut a quick glance at Grace, but she didn't even notice him, her attention fully riveted on the accountant. She still looked just as lovely as he remembered. Older, of course, but just as beautiful. More so, if that was even possible. He'd heard stories about her illustrious career at one of those Silicon Valley ride-sharing apps, probably raking in the millions. He wondered how long she'd be in town. Not long, probably. Long enough to attend her dad's funeral, and to give the family business the once-over, before going back to her high-flying life on the West Coast.

He wondered if she'd remember him. Probably not. It was such a long time ago now. Twenty-four years. He hadn't heard about her being married. Though most likely she was seeing someone. Some high-powered exec just like herself.

He took a left turn where she took a right, and he was sure their paths would never cross again. And that was probably for the best.

CHAPTER 12

Steven watched the Wheeler sisters pass through his lobby again and frowned. "I'd have thought they would have left by now," he told Hazel, who was fumbling with a packet of cigarettes. She was on her break, and couldn't wait to light one up. Even though she looked old enough to be Steven's grandmother, in actual fact she was probably in her sixties, but smoking for over forty years had had a deleterious effect on her skin, giving it the consistency of dark leather.

"They're selling the business," Hazel said. "The Wheeler family is selling the business to some foreign investor and pretty soon they're going to kick us all out."

"Some Saudi prince, you think?" Steven speculated. "Or the Chinese?"

"My money is on the Saudis," said Hazel. "They've got the moolah, and they're always interested in snapping up another piece of prime real estate."

"I wouldn't mind working for a Saudi prince," said Steven. "It might even be an improvement. At least they might invest some money in a new swimming pool."

"Or a decent spa," Hazel growled, nervously tapping the counter with one of her long fingernails. Like talons, they looked as if they could do some serious damage. "Cole is a great handyman, but even he can't keep working miracles."

Hazel was right. The spa needed a complete renovation, as did most other parts of the resort. Guests kept complaining about malfunctioning taps and showers, and parts of the infrastructure were really starting to show their age. At least they had decent wi-fi.

"I don't like it," said Hazel as her dark eyes followed the Wheeler sisters as they made their way back to their dad's office. "I don't like it at all. This place is going down the tubes, and the Wheelers are letting it happen." She narrowed her eyes. "The good old days are gone, sonny boy. And they're never coming back."

"I'm afraid there's nothing we can do about that, old thing," said Steven.

Hazel cut him a nasty glance. "Who are you calling old, you young fool?"

"It's generally accepted as a term of endearment, sweetie."

"Hm," Hazel grumbled, and then stalked off to enjoy her smoke.

Steven released a deep sigh. The atmosphere was approaching subzero temperatures, and he wasn't sure any Saudi prince, no matter how deep his pockets, could bring back that old pizzazz. Maybe Hazel was right, and the good days were gone indeed. Well, at least he'd lived them, and enjoyed them. No one could take that away from him. He plastered an ingratiating smile on his face to welcome his next guest, a pretty young woman who was wearing an oversized straw hat, and equally oversized dark glasses.

Another celebrity? He studied her for a moment, but didn't think he'd ever seen her before. So not a celebrity. Still, she was a guest, and so entitled to the same excellent service all their guests received.

"How may I help you?" he asked in his usual unctuous tones. They might all lose their jobs at any moment, but that wasn't going to stop him from doing his job to perfection, the way he'd always done it.

* * *

Olivia Hill glanced up at the receptionist, and clocked his smile and his kind demeanor. Automatically she reciprocated his smile with one of her own, though when she signed the register, she experienced a momentary twinge of alarm. Her hand froze over the document.

"Everything all right?" asked the receptionist solicitously.

"You… practice discretion, don't you?" she asked.

"Of course," said the young man smoothly. He leaned in. "If I were to tell you about the celebrities who've stayed here, with no one being any the wiser, you'd be surprised, Miss…" He glanced down at the document. "Hill?"

She nodded. "You don't recognize me, do you?"

"Even if I did, mum's the word," said the guy. She glanced at his name tag.

"If anyone calls or asks for me, please don't tell them I'm staying here… Steven."

"Like I said, mum's the word," said the receptionist. He gave her a look of concern. "You're not in any trouble, are you? I mean, I don't want to pry, but I'm a very good listener, and I'm also very discreet—two things that come with the job."

"I'm fine," she said, but still felt reassured enough to finally sign.

She proceeded in the direction of her room, and the

moment she had entered, got rid of the hat and the sunglasses, and sank down on the bed. For a moment she just sat there, wondering if she'd done the right thing. Then she closed her eyes and let herself fall back. She enjoyed the gentle bounce of the mattress, and knowing that no one knew where she was somehow gave her a measure of comfort. Well, her parents knew, of course, but they would never tell.

Suddenly her phone buzzed. Startled, she took it out, and glanced at the display. Her heart rate instantly spiked, and for a moment she had trouble breathing. But as the buzzing stopped, she found that she'd been holding her breath all the while. They had that effect on her, the bastards.

She hesitated for a moment, then added the number to her list of blocked numbers, and threw the phone down as if it might bite.

She couldn't lie down after that, so she jumped up and walked over to the window, where she proceeded to stare out at the glittering waves. Birds were dipping down, and she could see people swimming in the surf. And slowly but gradually, her breathing returned to normal, and so did her heartbeat. So much so that she took a deep breath, and smelled that lovely scent of brine in the air.

At least they wouldn't bother her again.

As she closed her eyes, she wondered what the rest of her life would look like. Her dreams, her hopes, her future—all gone now. Destroyed by one man.

As the lead singer of OceanPeak One, the popular choir of the OceanPeak Church, Olivia hadn't merely built what might be called a career. She'd built a life in service of a higher purpose, or at least what she thought was a higher purpose. A religious girl, singing for God had always been her dream, and so when she got the chance to join Ocean-

Peak One, she felt she'd arrived home. She was finally at the place she was supposed to be, answering a higher calling, and devoting her not inconsiderable talent to her Lord and Savior.

She'd traveled the world with OceanPeak One, singing in front of crowds of thousands, and spreading His message to millions. She'd sung on albums that had shot to number one on the charts, as unlikely as that might have seemed at the time, and in a way had become a star, not by design but because she had the talent, through her unique voice, of touching people's hearts.

She didn't care about all of that, though. The adulation. The applause. The cheers. The only thing she cared about was spreading His Word.

The band she fronted, OceanPeak One, consisted of a bunch of artists just like herself: not interested in money or glory or fame, but happy to spread the word.

And for ten years, that had been her whole life, and a wonderful, magical life it was. OceanPeak One had taken her across the globe, and she'd met so many amazing people along the way—fellow travelers, just like her.

One man who'd made a deep impression on her was Pastor Frank. A charismatic pastor, he led the LA chapter of the church, and his weekly mass drew in thousands. There was something about him that made you want to be close to him, and she couldn't count the number of times she'd breathlessly listened to his sermons, even watching them on YouTube over and over again, allowing his gentle voice and his compassionate words to touch her heart.

Until one night, in a drunken stupor, that wonderful Pastor Frank had groped her and had tried to have sex with her. Too shocked to respond at first, he'd half undressed her by the time she understood what was going on. And it had taken a firm knee to the groin for the revered pastor to understand his attentions weren't appreciated.

She'd hesitated a long time about filing a complaint, but when she finally did, much to her surprise her testimony hadn't brought along an investigation into the conduct and behavior of the pastor, but instead had seen her being removed from her position as frontwoman of OceanPeak One, and asked to leave the church.

Apparently Pastor Frank was more important to the church than a mere singer.

Since then, other women had come forward, and had privately expressed to her similar experiences. Turns out Pastor Frank was a womanizer of the first order, and had been cheating on his wife and betraying his family for years, with full knowledge of his church superiors. But since he was such a major draw, and such a figurehead of the church, his behavior was silently condoned, and anyone threatening his position was either bought off or silenced.

They'd offered her a cash sum if she kept quiet, which she'd refused. And then they'd told her that if she ever opened her mouth again about what happened, they'd not only kick her out of the church, but her entire family.

She couldn't let that happen. Her mom and dad's whole life was in that church. Being excommunicated would end them.

So she'd backed off, and had left without kicking up a fuss.

And now here she was, wondering what was next for her.

After a lifetime in the church, that was a hard one.

All her friends were in that church—her whole life. Without it, who was she? She had no idea. She had nowhere to go. No friends, since all of her friends had mysteriously disappeared the moment she was dropped from OceanPeak One.

She took a step back and caught her reflection in the window.

Slim, with fair hair and pale eyes, she found a woman staring back at her with haunted eyes. A woman who faced an uncertain future. She reached out to her reflection. "Who are you?" she whispered.

CHAPTER 13

In the next room, Tim Deutch was talking to his mom.

"Yes, Mom, I'm fine," he assured her. "I'm at a resort in the Hamptons. No, I'm not making a new movie. I'm on holiday." He listened for a moment and smiled. His mom was his number-one fan. And contrary to some of his other fans, she didn't want to own a piece of him, or rip his shirt off his back to get it. "Yes, I'll take good care of myself. I'm just taking a break." He wanted to confess to her it had all been too much, and he was tired of the celebrity circus. But she wouldn't understand. She wasn't into the celebrity cult that held so many people in its grip. She didn't even read the gossip magazines, knowing how many lies they spread.

"I want you to know I support any decision you make, Tim," said his mom.

"Thanks, Mom," he said, though he had no idea what decision that would be, since he hadn't made it yet. Though it sounded like his mom had some inkling.

"And if you want to come home, your room is always here, and your bed is made."

"I know, Mom," he said. "But I'm fine here for now. Nobody knows where I am, and it's going to do me some good to be incognito for a while."

He heard a male voice shout something in the background, and his mom said, "Your dad says hi, and to make sure you don't turn vegan, like the rest of those Hollywood stars."

"I very much doubt all Hollywood stars are vegan," he said with a laugh. "But thanks for the advice."

After he'd hung up, immediately his phone rang out its tune, and so he picked up immediately, figuring his mom had forgotten to tell him something. Instead, it was his agent.

"Timmy!" Steve cried, clearly happy to finally get him on the line. "You disappeared on me, buddy. Tell me what's happening."

"Nothing's happening," said Tim, his mood souring quickly. Steve was the last person he wanted to talk to right now. "I'm taking a couple of days off is all."

"Where are you?"

"On vacation," he said.

"Yeah, but where? See, the thing is that I need you in a meeting tomorrow morning at Warner's. They're setting up a new movie based on Monchhichi."

"The doll?"

"Yeah, the doll. Toys are hot, buddy boy. Just look at Lego, or Barbie, or Transformers. We could be looking at another billion-dollar franchise here!"

"Look, Steve..." Tim began.

"They want you to play the lead Monchhichi. The big Monchhichi. The top monkey. I think this is going to be great. I've already got them up to twenty-three."

"Million?" he asked, in spite of himself.

"No, M&M's. Of course million!"

"I don't know," he said.

"Just think about it. But not too long. You have to be in that meeting tomorrow. You're not too far away, are you? I could send a plane to pick you up if you want."

"I'm sorry, but I can't make it to the meeting, Steve."

"Fine. No problem. We'll reschedule. How about next Wednesday?"

"I'll let you know," said Tim, eager to get rid of the agent.

There was a pause, then Steve said, "Everything all right, Timmy? I don't know, but you sound kinda down. You're not depressed or anything, are you?"

"I'm just tired," he said. "Been doing too much for a long time and I need a break."

"Hey, I hear you," said Steve. "We all need a break sometimes. So you have some fun, and let me know when you're ready to get back in the saddle. And in the meantime I'll send the proposal for the Monchhichi thing your way."

"Okay, thanks."

"Take a look and let me know what you think."

"Will do, Steve."

After he got off the horn, he found that his head was a mess. Somehow Steve always had that effect on him. Made him decide things that he didn't want to do. Which was probably a hallmark of an effective agent, he assumed.

They'd already had a discussion about his future a couple of weeks ago, when Tim had told him he was thinking about a change of pace. No more blockbuster movies for a while. Maybe some indie productions. Or some theater. He wanted to be an actor again, not some dog doing tricks in front of a green screen. That wasn't the life he'd chosen, and if he continued to go down that road he was afraid he'd burn out sooner rather than later.

But Steve had argued that they had to strike while the iron was hot. An actor's career could be over in a flash. One wrong move and you were out. And besides, he was an A-lister now, and if he was going to do indie productions it would jeopardize his quote—and Steve's commission—and he might never get back on top. And he'd named a couple of actors who'd made the same kind of money Tim was making, actors who had disappeared from the scene, and some Tim had never even heard of. One of their movies had bombed, or some scandal had destroyed their career. It certainly gave Tim food for thought.

"You can make that indie stuff later, when you're old and gray," Steve had said. "Right now is when you need to make money, baby. Just think of yourself as a football player. Those guys have a very short window of time in which to make enough money to last them for the rest of their lives. Three years, Timmy. Three years! That's the average length of an NFL player's career. So let's make hay while the sun shines, okay buddy boy? Now where did I put that Coca-Cola contract?"

Sounds of kids playing in the pool drifted into his room through the open window and suddenly he wanted to join them. Swim a couple of laps and clear his head. So he grabbed a towel and headed out. The pool probably wasn't a good idea, especially if it was filled with kids, the primary audience for his movie output. But the ocean was just as good—even better. And so he pulled his ball cap deep over his eyes, put on his sunglasses, lowered his head and walked out.

CHAPTER 14

Grace and her sisters were sitting on the terrace overlooking the ocean when Grace thought she saw a familiar figure. A guy with a ball cap pulled down low and oversized sunglasses was walking in the direction of the beach. The way he walked rang a bell, though she couldn't immediately place him. But since she had bigger fish to fry, she focused her attention on what Jill was saying.

"Honestly, I don't think we have time to find a general manager. That could take weeks, or months, and in the meantime the resort needs to be run. I mean, the previous general manager neglected the job for years, and now he's gone. And his assistant manager just left us to join the competition. We need someone now."

"You're right," said Grace. "We need someone today, not a couple of weeks from now."

"What about Mom?" Lauren suggested.

"What about her?" said Grace.

"She's got experience running things, hasn't she?"

"Yeah, Mom runs that flower show," Jill said. "Or at least she used to."

"And her book club," Lauren pointed out.

"Running a flower show or a book club is not the same as running a resort," said Grace as she took a sip from her soda. No more alcohol for her. They needed to keep a clear head if they wanted to keep this ship from sinking.

"Can't we offer Michele some kind of incentive to stay on board?" said Lauren. "Promise her the general manager position, with a substantial pay raise, or some kind of bonus?"

At the mention of the word 'bonus' Grace winced. She'd hoped to land a nice fat bonus when it became clear Polys was letting her go. But instead they'd threatened to sue her for damaging the company's reputation. So no bonus.

"I don't know," she said. "Michele doesn't strike me as the kind of woman who'd stick around for a pay raise or a bonus. She seemed determined to walk away from the Hampton Cove. And besides, I'm pretty sure we'll never be able to match what the Argent is offering her, both in terms of money and career prospects."

"Yeah, I guess so," said Lauren.

"No, I think we need to think outside of the box here," said Grace. "Or inside the box, if you will."

"What are you talking about?" said Jill, giving her a look of suspicion.

"First off, we need to get in touch with this mystery investor Nicolas mentioned. And find out what his plans are."

"Nicolas said he's a silent partner, and he's not going to get involved in the day-to-day business of running the resort," Lauren pointed out.

"True, but he might have some ideas. And since it now looks like we're stuck with this guy, we might as well find out what those ideas are."

"Okay, so we get in touch with our mystery investor," said

Jill. "And then what? He's not going to magically spirit a new general manager out of his hat, is he?"

"Which is why we need to step up ourselves."

"Step up ourselves? You're talking in riddles, sis," said Jill.

"We're all agreed that we need a manager yesterday, right?" Two heads bobbed up and down. "And who knows this place better than we do?"

Jill gave her a frown. "You're not suggesting that we run the resort?"

"That's exactly what I'm suggesting. I have some management experience, so I could step into the role of general manager for the time being—until we find a new one. Jill, you'd make a great fitness coach—and yoga teacher. And you, Lauren, would be an excellent customer relations person. So between the three of us we could fill these three positions—just for now. Couple of weeks, tops."

She could tell her words had struck a chord. "There's some logic in what you're saying," said Lauren slowly. "Though I'm not too sure about the customer relations thing. I mean, I haven't worked in years, honey."

"You're a mother and a wife—you've run your household for years. I say you've got all the experience you need to deal with difficult customers."

"It's true that I know my way around a fitness club," Jill admitted. "And I have given yoga lessons, so I could probably step in and take over from the previous person. But are you sure taking on the manager job isn't something of a stretch for you? I mean, especially after everything you've been through at Polys?"

But Grace waved an airy hand. "How hard can it be? If I can handle being a VP at one of the country's biggest ride-sharing companies, I think running a resort should be a breeze. And besides, it's only for a couple of weeks. Until whoever will be in charge next steps in."

"Okay, I guess I can live with that," said Lauren. "When do we start?"

Her sister actually looked happy about the prospect of rolling up her sleeves and tackling this new challenge. Jill, too, looked moderately excited.

"I mean, it's not as if we're going anywhere anytime soon," said Jill.

"No more adventures in the Far East for you?" asked Lauren.

"Not a chance," said Jill decidedly. "I've had my fill of gurus and enlightenment and spiritual journeys for a while. I'm staying put. At least for now."

Her two sisters smiled at that. Jill had never been able to stay put. Not even for a while. So they'd see how long she managed to stick around this time.

"How about you?" asked Lauren. "When some headhunter comes knocking, and offers you a job as CEO for some startup, are you going to turn them down?"

"Absolutely," said Grace, and she actually meant it, too. She'd had it with having to deal with the male ego on a daily basis, and having to struggle against a toxic work environment, thinking the big paycheck made everything all right. It didn't make everything all right, and she knew that now. She'd allowed people to overstep her boundaries for far too long, and needed time to lick her wounds.

"Aren't you going to miss New York?" asked Jill. She had directed her question at Lauren. "Or the kids?"

"Yeah, and what if Jack suddenly decides a career in rock music isn't for him after all?" said Grace. "And he comes crawling back to you?"

"He won't," said Lauren quietly. She looked a little sad as she said it, Grace thought. Obviously she didn't think Jack would come back to her.

"Even if he did come back, I wouldn't take him if I were you," said Jill.

Lauren shrugged. "I had the impression Jack made up his mind when he told me he wanted a divorce. And it wasn't about pursuing a career in music. I think he's been thinking about this for a long time. Leaving me, I mean."

"Oh, honey."

"He had everything in place. A divorce lawyer, a proposal for the apartment, what to do about the twins. My impression was that he had this planned for months, maybe even longer. And I think I can pinpoint the exact moment he decided to put his plan into action: when the twins went off to college. As long as they were still at home, he wouldn't have done it. The moment it was just the two of us, he felt he no longer needed to be there for them, and so he called quits on our marriage."

"You don't know that, Lauren," said Grace, putting a hand on her sister's arm.

"No, I don't. But that's what I think happened. And I'd be very much surprised if it wasn't."

They were all silent for a moment. It really was extraordinary: Lauren had been dumped by Jack, Jill by her fraudulent guru, and Grace by Jay Polys. And then she was forgetting about Mom, who was living through the biggest disgrace of them all.

"I'm worried about Mom," she now said.

"Yeah, me too," Jill chimed in.

"When I asked her to come with us this morning she said she's never leaving the house again," said Lauren. "She looked really depressed when she said it."

"God, Mom would be so good at doing the PR for the resort," said Grace. She'd already put on her general manager's cap, and was thinking up ways and means of putting the place on the right track again.

"Let's give her some time," said Lauren. "She's had a big, nasty shock."

"Yeah, let's give Mom some time, and some space," Jill agreed.

"Good thing we're all here right now," said Grace. "We can be there for her when she needs us."

And it was obvious to the three of them that their beloved mother needed them now more than ever.

CHAPTER 15

Bea had made an effort to get up when she'd heard the girls pottering about, but after they'd left, she'd gone straight back to bed. For some reason she simply couldn't be bothered. No one to see, nowhere to go, so why get dressed and get ready? Ready for what? Her so-called friends were probably all laughing behind her back right now, sharing juicy gossip about silly Bea who was cheated on by her husband with her best friend for years and didn't even know about it.

The fact of the matter was that she felt ashamed. Ashamed and humiliated, and if it was up to her she'd never show her face in town again. In fact, she thought as she lay there in bed and stared at the ceiling, she might move to a place where no one knew her. Some nice coastal town where she could start over. She would sell the house, and maybe sell the resort, and start over. She wasn't too old to start over, was she? She was only sixty-two, after all. People had started over who were older than she was, right? Maybe she'd even find new romance.

She closed her eyes. Who was she kidding? She was old.

Too old for romance. And besides, she didn't want to find romance. She wasn't interested in men anymore, not after what Johnny had put her through.

And so she turned over and gradually drifted off to sleep again.

She woke up when a door slammed downstairs, and feet sounded on the stairs. The door opened and when she looked up, she saw that Jill had walked in.

"Mom!" said Jill. "What's wrong?"

"Nothing's wrong," she said. "I'm just having a lazy day."

"You should get up and get dressed," said her youngest daughter as she took a seat on the bed next to her. "Have you taken a shower?"

She shook her head as Jill brushed a strand of hair from her brow.

"Take a shower and get dressed," Jill advised. "You'll feel better if you do."

"I know," said Bea. She knew she'd feel better if she got up and got dressed. But what was the point? You got dressed to go places, to do stuff. She didn't have anywhere to go, and nothing to do. So she might as well stay where she was. "How did things go at the resort?"

"Not so good," said Jill. "Did you know that Dad had let things slide the last couple of years?"

She frowned. "What do you mean? He was going to work every day."

"No, he wasn't. I don't know where he went, but according to Michele—who quit today, by the way—he hardly showed his face there anymore. She told us she was running that place all by herself for at least the past five years."

"Five years," Bea murmured. "Do you think that's when the affair started?"

"I still can't believe he would do this, and with Aunt Juda, of all people."

Bea gave her daughter a kind look. "I think it's time you stopped calling her Aunt Juda, sweetie."

"I know. It's just that... Well, we've always considered her like family, and now all of a sudden..."

There was more noise on the stairs, and Jill's sisters walked in.

"Mom! What's wrong!" Lauren called out, and streaked to her side.

"I'm fine," Bea said. "Just don't feel like getting up, that's all."

"Mom is feeling under the weather," Jill explained.

Lauren put her hand to Bea's forehead. "You're a little hot. Should we call a doctor?"

"No!" said Bea. "I'm telling you I'm fine. There's nothing wrong with me." Apart from the fact that she was going to move to the other side of the country. Either that, or she'd lock herself up in this house and never leave again.

"Did you tell her about the resort?" asked Grace. "What we decided?"

"What did you decide?" asked Bea, though she wasn't really interested. The resort could go to hell, along with Johnny and 'Auntie' Juda and all the rest.

"Michele quit, and a bunch of other people," Grace explained. "And Nicolas told us that there are some financial difficulties, owing to the fact that Dad spent money he should have used to invest into the business to buy fancy cars and expensive gifts for Juda and exclusive vacations in St Barts and Monaco."

"God," said Bea. Just when you thought things couldn't get any worse, they did.

"Nicolas said he used the resort like his personal ATM machine," said Lauren, as she gently stroked her mother's hair. "And now we're on the verge of going broke. Luckily Dad also found an outside investor, who's going to keep us afloat."

"An outside investor? What outside investor?"

Lauren shrugged. "Some rich guy, interested in diversifying his portfolio or something. He's going to be taking a hands-off approach, though."

"So your dad actually sold the family business?" She sat up, feeling furious all over again. "The business my dad set up and turned into a success story?"

"Looks like," said Jill.

"Which isn't necessarily a bad thing, Mom," said Grace. "I mean, at some point it's probably a good idea to bring in some investment money so you can expand the business. Nicolas gave us a tour of the facilities, and I have to say the place looks run down. It's going to take a sizable cash injection to bring it up to standard again. The rooms need renovating, the pool area needs to be redone..."

"It does look dilapidated," said Lauren. "Neglected is the best way to describe it."

"If Johnny hadn't been chasing Juda for the past five years, and had kept his eye on the ball like he promised my dad, this wouldn't have happened," Bea said as she rubbed her face. "Oh, God. This just keeps getting worse, doesn't it?"

"The good news is that we're going to step in and keep the place afloat for the time being," said Grace. "Jill and Lauren and I have decided to take over the positions that need to be filled, until we can find new people to replace us."

"What do you mean?"

"It's just temporary, Mom," said Lauren. "But Michele quit this morning, and also the girl who ran the fitness and yoga center, and the customer service person. And since it's not easy to find replacements on such short notice, we're going to be stepping in for now. Grace as general manager, Jill as the fitness and yoga instructor, and me in charge of customer relations."

"But... don't you have to be in New York, honey?"

Lauren shook her head sadly. "We're selling the apartment. We have to, since I don't have the kind of money to buy Jack's share of the place. And Jack wants to sell. He needs the money. He's moving to Austin, I think he said. Or was it Nashville? He wants to invest in his music career."

"But what about the twins?"

"They'll be fine. I already talked to them and they understand."

"And what about you?" asked Bea, turning to Grace. "What about your career?"

"What career?" Grace scoffed. "I don't have a career anymore. When you get fired for being in violation of the ethics code, no one is clamoring to hire you. In fact you might say I'm unhirable right now." She shook her head, and judging from the pained expression on her face she was still having a hard time dealing with what had transpired at Polys. "No, that part of my life is over, Mom. I'll just have to move on."

"But isn't running a resort below your skill level? I mean, you could do so much more."

Grace put on a brave face. "It'll be fine. A nice change of pace. I've been working my ass off for so long that it'll be good for me to take a break. Get some perspective and decide what I want to do with the rest of my life." She shrugged. "It's freeing, you know, in a sense. Like, I could write a book now or something."

"I didn't know you wanted to be a writer."

"No, I don't, but it's a possibility now. Everything is possible. Absolutely everything. Which is wonderful when you think about it. Absolutely great."

She didn't look so great, but Bea decided to shut up, lest

she made her oldest daughter cry. "And what about you?" she asked Jill. "Are you sure you won't get bored here? It's not Goa, or Nepal." Or wherever her youngest daughter's quest for enlightenment had taken her in the past couple of years.

"It's fine," Jill assured her. And it was clear that she, too, was going to need some time to lick her wounds, and to get over this guy who'd dumped her.

"Okay, and now you really have to get up, Mom," said Lauren, taking her by the arm. "Take a long, hot shower, get dressed, and you'll see that you'll feel much better."

And more to please her girls than for herself, Bea allowed Lauren to throw off the covers and escort her to the bathroom. She stopped short of allowing her daughters to escort her into the shower, though. There were limits to what she was prepared to do to make them feel reassured about their mother's state of mind.

Once she was in the shower, though, with the hot water massaging her scalp, she had to admit Lauren was right. She was feeling better, even if for only five minutes.

She still wasn't going to leave the house, though. But it was nice to have the girls there. Without them, the house would have felt empty, especially since she hadn't heard from any of her friends since the incident. Not a phone call, not a visit, not even a WhatsApp message. She was officially a social pariah. Only Juda had been calling—and calling and calling and calling. But she wasn't talking to her.

CHAPTER 16

Tim was sitting at the bar, nursing his drink, and quietly hoping no one would recognize him. He'd chosen the far corner of the bar, and was wearing his now customary disguise: sunglasses and a ball cap, even though the sunglasses might be overdoing it at night, and might actually draw more attention to him.

Still, so far no one had walked up to him. No kids had asked him to strike a pose, or their mom and dad mugging it up for a selfie. So it was all to the good.

He hadn't actually wanted to come out tonight, but the band that was playing was supposed to be pretty good, and besides, once they were playing, no one would pay any attention to the members of the audience. He could simply disappear into the crowd. Odd, that. When he was younger, he never wanted to disappear into the crowd. He wanted to stand out. Stand on stage and perform and entertain. So where had it all gone wrong?

He checked his phone, and saw that his agent had left three messages, asking him if he'd had a chance to look over the proposal. He groaned. The last thing he needed right now was to think about his next blockbuster. So he put away his phone and sipped from his drink. There apparently was some kind of delay, for the band, which should have been playing already, still hadn't arrived on stage. He hoped they would. Steven, the receptionist guy, had told him they were amazing.

He glanced in the direction of the stage, and when he looked back, he was startled to see that some guy had taken the next seat and was staring intently at him. Uh-oh.

"I know you," said the guy.

"I doubt it," said Tim, lowering his head.

"You were in that movie, weren't you? You're that actor."

"I'm afraid you're mistaking me for someone else, sir," he said, as politely as he could.

"I never forget a face," said the stranger. "Or a name. You're Tim Deutch."

"I can assure you that I'm not," Tim insisted, hoping the guy would just leave.

"Don't worry," said the man. "I can keep a secret." He gave him a conspiratorial wink. "You're trying to have a good time —trying not to be recognized. I get that."

"Great," said Tim.

"So you are him!" said the guy.

Tim groaned. "I would appreciate it if you could keep your voice down."

"Look, I don't want to cause any trouble," said the guy, who must have sensed that Tim was less than pleased to see him. "But I'm actually in the movie business myself." He slid a card across the bar. "Howard Jucha."

Tim frowned as he studied the card. "You're a producer?"

"Yeah, my company mainly specializes in small indie productions. Nothing major like you. Still, I won a couple of awards."

"I know your work," said Tim. "Some great stuff."

"Why, thanks. Coming from you that's a major compliment." He studied Tim for a moment. "I've always wondered why you don't do smaller productions. You've got the talent. You could totally make it work."

"I've actually been wanting to act in some of the projects you're involved in," said Tim, his interest piqued now that the guy obviously wasn't a selfie-demanding fan.

"So why don't you?"

He would have told the producer that he was engaged in an ongoing struggle to convince his agent, but since that wasn't anyone's business, he just shrugged. "I guess I just haven't found the right project yet."

"Well, let me correct that right now," said Howard. "I've got a great little production coming up that would be right up your alley. Here, let me show you." He'd taken out his phone and proceeded to show Tim some snippets from a script he was working on. And after he gave him the logline and pitched the project to him, Tim had to admit it sounded exactly like the kind of thing he wanted to do.

"Could you send me the script?" he finally asked.

"Sure. Who's your agent?"

"Just send it to me," he suggested. "I want to take a look for myself."

This surprised Howard a great deal, as that wasn't the way things were usually done. And Tim thought the other man must have sensed what the issue was, for he said, "If you wanted to, you could always sell it to your agent as a passion project. Or as a favor to a friend."

"But we don't know each other."

Howard flashed a grin. "Your agent doesn't know that."

Tim smiled. "I'll give it some thought," he promised. And he actually meant it. He'd been dreaming of doing a smaller movie like this for a long time. Now it might actually happen. He could always combine it with his regular high-profile stuff, couldn't he? There were actors who did that kind of thing all the time. They were popular actors, A-listers, but also took on smaller, more challenging projects, with interesting parts. Why couldn't he be like them?

He watched as Howard headed in the direction of the stage, and saw him talk to a guy hoisting a camera on his shoulder. Looked like they were going to film the show. So maybe that was what the holdup was about.

He turned back to the bar, and for the next few minutes studied the script Howard had sent him. It looked good. Right up his alley, just like the producer had said. Now all he had to do was convince his agent that it was a good idea.

CHAPTER 17

A couple of bar seats down from Tim, Olivia was gazing out across the crowd. Once upon a time she'd been the one they would all be waiting for. To get up on stage and do her thing. Now she was in the crowd, waiting for the show to begin.

She actually felt relaxed. Happy that she was just an onlooker. Though if she was honest, she knew she was fooling herself. She loved being up there on that stage. To look out across a sea of people, singing along with her. The energy, the excitement—it was such a high—such a buzz. There was nothing like it. And to think she would never be that person again just served to depress her.

She looked up when a young man joined her. He had long sideburns and a stylishly coiffed beard and was staring at her intently. "Olivia Hill?" he asked. "You're Olivia Hill, right?"

For a moment she wanted to deny it, but obviously this guy knew her, so she gave him a gamely smile and said, "Yep, that's me."

"Oh, great. My name is Shawn Dree. I play drums for Due

Course. I thought I recognized you. Big fan, Miss Hill. Big, big fan."

"Thanks. Likewise," she said, well pleased to meet a fellow musician. "I love Due Course. You're about to start your show?"

The man grimaced. "That was the plan, but our lead singer Julie is a no-show. So looks like the gig is canceled."

"Oh, no. What do you think happened?"

He leaned against the bar and dragged a weary hand through his shaggy mane. "She might have quit—I don't know. She's been unhappy with the band for a while now, and has been thinking about leaving. Looks like she finally did. Though she could have told us before we drove all the way out here and set up."

"That's too bad," said Olivia sympathetically. "And you don't have a backup?"

"Mikey can sing some, but obviously not as well as Julie." He shook his head. "It just wouldn't be the same. Pretty sure our audience wouldn't appreciate it."

"You never know. There have been bands that lost their lead singer and then the new singer turned out to be even better than the original one."

"I know. But those are extremely rare cases," said Shawn, who looked a little down, Olivia thought. Then his face lit up. "Say, why don't you sing with us?"

"Me!" she laughed. "Oh, no, I couldn't."

"You said you like our stuff."

"Well, I do. But..."

"Just a couple of songs. The playlist is five songs, but we could cut the set down to two or three, due to circumstances. People will understand. But then at least they won't have come out for nothing."

"I don't know..." she said. "I don't know the lyrics. Or the melody. I'd suck."

"You could never suck, Olivia," said Shawn fervently. "You're simply great."

She laughed shyly. He was such a charmer she was almost tempted to say yes. But it was too soon.

"Or we could play one of your songs," he suggested.

She shook her head. "I'm never singing those songs again —ever."

He seemed taken aback by her vehemence, which she regretted as soon as the words were out of her mouth. Her problems were her own, personal issue. Nothing she wanted to blab about to others. "I'm on vacation," she explained.

"Yeah, I hear you," he said, then proceeded to look like a lamb led to the slaughter. She felt for him, she really did.

"Okay, so maybe one song." She suggested a song that was one of her favorites, and which she'd sung so many times she knew it by heart.

Shawn immediately perked up. "That would work," he said.

"But I'll just do the one," she warned him. "No encores."

"Absolutely." He gave her a look of such gratitude she had to laugh. He had a sort of puppy dog thing going for him, which made it hard to say no. "Let me introduce you to the rest of the band. They'll be honored that the great Olivia Hill has agreed to perform with us tonight."

When all was said and done, she sang no less than five songs with Due Course. Turns out she did know a couple of their songs, and the parts she didn't, they simply improvised. And she had to admit it felt great to be up there again. In fact it was exactly what she needed after the terrible events that had transpired.

In the front row, an older couple was sitting, clapping and obviously loving the mini-concert. And as she saw the look of happiness on the woman's face, she knew that this was what she was made for. This was her destiny.

* * *

HEATHER DAVIS WAS ALMOST MOVED to tears as the band concluded their show. "What a voice," she told her husband, who was seated next to her in the front row. "She just gives me the chills."

"I know her," said Terry. "Or at least I think so."

"She's not their regular singer, is she?"

"No, a replacement," said Terry, taking out his phone.

On stage, they were already starting to disassemble the set. She loved the entertainment at the resort. They always had the best shows and the best concerts. Like tonight, with a band that had exceeded her expectations.

"Here, this is her," said Terry, showing her a video of a concert. He was right. It was the same singer, her voice and her stage presence were simply unmistakable.

"She's going to make it big," said Heather. And she deserved it. She definitely had the talent. She watched as the singer, Olivia Hill was her name, walked off stage, and in the direction of the bar. She was accompanied by a young man with remarkable sideburns and a funky-looking beard and mustache. She looked radiant, and he looked happy. And suddenly a pang of heartache shot through her. She and Terry had been like that once: young and happy, their whole lives ahead of them. And now, when they were at the end, she wondered where the years had gone to. Fifty years they were married now. Fifty wonderful, happy years.

"Do you want something to drink?" asked Terry.

But she shook her head. They couldn't afford it. In fact they couldn't even afford to stay at the resort, and should have left already. But where would they go? They'd lost the house, lost every bit of savings they had, and their bank account was empty. The only money they had was the money in their wallets, which wasn't much.

The concert had been Terry's idea. Heather hadn't even wanted to come. She wanted to leave—not face the embarrassment of having to admit to the resort management that they wouldn't be able to pay their bill.

But Terry felt they deserved a fun night. A night they could forget their financial troubles, and simply enjoy themselves. Just like they had before.

And she had enjoyed herself. Olivia Hill's talent had made her forget just for a few moments the kind of trouble they were in. But now that the show was over, it all came back to her—even more powerfully than before. They were broke. Dead broke.

"Let me buy you a drink," Terry insisted. "They'll put it on the tab."

"I don't think that's a good idea, Terry." She lowered her voice. "We can't afford it," she whispered.

He shrugged. "We're in a hole, Heather. So let's dig a little deeper. I mean, what does it matter now?"

There was a certain logic in what her husband was saying. But it just wouldn't be right. They couldn't take advantage of these people. They were their friends. So she got up. "No," she said decidedly. "Let's go for a walk instead."

And so they ended up walking along the beach. The sound of the gently crashing surf, and the silence of the evening soon made her anxiety dissipate. They sank down on the sand and looked out across the darkening expanse of water.

"Did you see that guy kiteboarding this afternoon?" asked Terry.

"A real daredevil," said Heather with a smile.

"I wouldn't mind trying some of that," said her husband.

She laughed. "Honey, you'd crash and burn."

"I know, but I would have fun doing it. I'd feel alive."

He said it with a longing note in his voice, and she knew

what he meant. Ever since they'd been swindled out of their savings, they'd both been feeling stressed and down to such a degree that they couldn't think of anything else. Thoughts of how to get out of their predicament consumed every waking hour—and kept them up at night, which caused them to wake up exhausted in the morning, when the whole thing just started all over again. So kitesurfing and ending up crashing in the surf was one way of getting rid of that.

"It was my fault," said Terry, reiterating a recurring theme in their conversations.

"Don't say that," said Heather. "It wasn't your fault or mine." If it was anyone's fault, it was the guy who'd fleeced them and had stolen all of their money.

"If I hadn't—"

"Just stop, Terry. You couldn't have known."

"I know, but still…"

She rubbed his back. They might have been together for what felt like forever, but there was still genuine affection there. She loved this man—always had, always would. He couldn't have known this guy was a fraud. He'd been recommended to them by their own banker, for crying out loud. If you couldn't trust your banker, then who could you trust? Of course now it had transpired that the banker had been in on the scam, and was in prison along with the scammer.

"Sometimes I imagine just walking into the water," Terry suddenly said softly. "And just walking and walking, you know… and not come back."

She should have been alarmed, but oddly enough, she wasn't. "I've been thinking the same thing," she admitted.

"It would solve all of our problems, wouldn't it?"

"It would. It would solve them in one go."

They were both quiet for a moment, as they watched the water lapping at their feet. "They say it's quick. And painless."

"I don't know, Terry," she said, and suddenly shivered.

“One big breath and it’s all over,” he murmured.

She moved closer to him, and enjoyed the warmth of him against her. “Hold me?” she asked a little timidly. And when he put his arm across her shoulder, she leaned in. “Don’t you dare walk into that ocean, Terry Davis,” she said.

“I wouldn’t,” he promised. “Not without you anyway.”

CHAPTER 18

Seven o'clock and the Wheeler family sat gathered around the breakfast table in the large family kitchen. As Grace brought a cup of strong coffee—made just the way she liked it—to her lips, she watched her mother over the rim of her cup. She didn't like what she saw. Mom looked drawn and thin, her hair was a mess, and she was wearing the same dressing gown she'd been wearing all day yesterday. She had the impression that the moment they left, Mom would go back to bed and not get out for the rest of the day.

"Maybe you could join us?" said Lauren, who'd noticed the same thing. "Mom?"

"Oh, no, absolutely not," said Mom, waving a determined hand. "I'm never setting foot in that resort ever again—never, never, never."

"But why? It's your place. You own it." Though maybe now she didn't. The exact terms of the contract Dad had signed with the new investor weren't immediately clear. Something they needed to look into these next couple of days.

"I don't care. I don't want people talking behind my back. Smiling to my face and then saying the worst kind of things about me when my back is turned. No way."

"Nobody is going to talk, Mom," said Jill, who sat cross-legged on her chair, a rare feat of lissomness Grace didn't think she was capable of. "I'm sure people will be happy to see you."

"Yes, Mom. Lots of familiar faces happy to see you," Lauren chimed in.

"I don't want to see any familiar faces," their mother insisted. "In fact I don't want to see any faces at all. Familiar or otherwise."

"You can't sit around here all day," said Grace. "You have to leave the house at some point."

Mom looked defiant. "Why? This is my house. If I want to stay here for the rest of my life and never meet a living soul that's my business, isn't it?"

"You're not seriously considering becoming a recluse, are you?" said Jill, smiling.

But Mom wasn't kidding. "I'll be like that Howard Hughes guy," she said. "I'll wear the same dress day in and day out and never show my face anywhere again. And I'll love it. And people will wonder what happened to me—if I'm alive or dead—and I just won't care. I won't care!" she insisted. "Or I could move away. Sell the house and move someplace nobody knows me. Mexico, maybe, or Belize. Plenty of perfectly nice places to live a happy life. Now wouldn't that be something?" She said it with a fervent sort of expression on her face.

The three sisters shared a look of concern.

"I'll open a tackle shop," said Mom, continuing her harangue. "I'll be the tackle shop lady, perfectly happy selling tackle and bait."

"Now what do you know about tackle, Mom?" said Jill.

"I can learn. How hard can it be?"

"Oh, Mom," said Grace, shaking her head. She got up and put her cup in the sink. Then on second thought, she quickly rinsed it and put it in the dish rack.

"There's something else we need to talk about," said Lauren. "Dad's funeral."

"I'm not going," Mom said immediately. "Wild horses couldn't drag me there."

Lauren looked stunned. "But..."

"No!" Mom almost cried. "Juda is going to be there, and Ruth and Jessica. And I don't want to see them. I don't want to see any of them ever again in my life."

Along with Juda, Ruth Gaynor and Jessica Vaca were Mom's best friends. The four of them had always been together, on the organizing committees of functions and charities and the flower show and a great many other social happenings. They were the backbone of Hampton Cove's social life, and now it looked as if that was all a thing of the past. Mom had resigned from every organization she was involved in.

"She was here, you know," said Mom quietly.

"Who was here, Mom?" asked Lauren carefully.

"Why, Juda, of course. She'd already left about a thousand messages, which I immediately deleted, of course, and so she decided to drop by the house, the two-timing floozie. I didn't open the door, of course. I could hear her rattling around outside, first trying the front door, then the back door, and finally looking in through the windows." She chuckled softly. "I had to hide behind the couch. I don't think she saw me, though. Took her long enough to get the message but finally she left."

"Oh, Mom," said Lauren with a sigh.

"Yeah, maybe it's time you finally had it out with the woman," said Jill.

Mom turned her head to her youngest so fast Grace could have sworn she heard a distinct creaking sound. "Never!" said Mom. "I'd rather poke myself in the eye with a hot poker than ever lay eyes on that woman again!"

Well, the message was certainly clear enough. Mom was leaving the country to open a tackle shop, and she was never going to talk to her old friends again. At least she was still talking to them, so there was that.

"Look, Mom," said Grace, deciding that perhaps the time had come for some straight talk. "I was also betrayed, and so was Jill, and Lauren. But you don't see us hiding in a corner somewhere, and talking about moving to Belize, do you?"

"You weren't betrayed by your husband *and* your best friend," Mom murmured. "You should have seen him, his hairy ass sticking out from between Juda's thin, white stalks for legs. Hers were shaved, of course. Perfectly shaped."

"God, Mom!" said Jill.

"When I close my eyes I can still see them. And then his sweaty, purple face as he just lay there, dead as a doornail." She shivered. "I gave that man the best years of my life, and this is how he thanked me. By boning my best friend and then dying on me. And you know the worst part? I didn't even get to have it out with him. Tell him how I felt about this rotten, rotten thing that he did. He just went and died on me, the coward. Taking the easy way out, just like he always did."

Grace wouldn't have called dying from a heart attack taking the easy way out, but she saw that her mom's lip was quivering dangerously, and decided to cancel her strong-worded speech for now. It didn't seem like the right time.

Instead she put her arms around her mom and gave her a

warm hug. "It's going to be all right," she told her wonderful, amazing mother.

Jill and Lauren joined her, and soon they were all hugging, with not a dry eye amongst them.

CHAPTER 19

Bea waved goodbye to the girls as they left for work, and thought how odd this all felt. Her three daughters living at home again, sharing their meals with her, and going to work at the resort the family had owned for three generations now. With Grace set to run the place, she would be the third generation in charge of the family business, after Johnny had run it since he'd taken over from Bea's dad.

Pity Johnny had almost managed to run the place into the ground. But then that just seemed par for the course, as he'd also succeeded in running their marriage into the ground, and in the end his own life.

The doctors had informed her that Johnny had suffered a massive cardiac arrest, and that three of the four arteries supplying blood to his heart had been blocked. They said he should have felt something about the malaise before. That there would have been warning signs. Chest pains, tiredness, and shortness of breath. And that if they'd caught it sooner, he might have been saved.

She hadn't admitted that she and Johnny had drifted apart

in recent years. She busy with her many social commitments, and Johnny always busy at the resort. Though as it now transpired, apparently he hadn't been busy at the resort, but elsewhere—occupying his time by enjoying a now-infamous tryst with Juda.

If they'd still been a normal couple, she would have seen the signs. She would have noticed if he was unusually tired, or suffering from chest pains. Apparently Juda hadn't noticed a thing until it was too late. And in that sense, Johnny had brought this upon himself. Maybe he had felt tired or in pain, but hadn't wanted to show it to Juda. A man always tries to put on a brave face for his mistress. Impress her. Show her how manly he is, and how virile. Johnny's wife might have caught the signs. Not his mistress, for he would have hidden his distress from her.

She wandered into the living room, feeling a little lost. It was true that she didn't want to go out. Didn't want to run the risk of bumping into Juda, or Ruth or Jessica. But she didn't feel comfortable walking around in her dressing gown all day either. So she walked up the stairs to take a shower and get dressed.

She loved having the girls home, she really did, but she wondered if she and Johnny hadn't somehow ruined their lives. Had their marriage been so bad that it had affected their daughters' chances of a happy marriage of their own?

Jill who kept running off to some faraway place to find 'enlightenment' and ended up falling for some creepy guru. Grace who got involved with her boss, and lost not only a career she'd worked so very hard to build, but any future prospects as well. And Lauren, whose husband turned out to be a jerk and a complete idiot.

Not exactly a great track record. And so she blamed herself. And Johnny. If only she'd picked a better husband, her three daughters might have done the same. Instead, they'd all been cheated out of a great life, maybe for good.

And on that sobering thought, she stepped into the shower.

* * *

AS THE NEW GENERAL MANAGER, Grace took over her dad's office. And after clearing away some of the junk that had gathered on his desk, and putting his golf trophies into a drawer, she stared out across her domain—as visible through the window, which offered a great view of the pool area—and wondered how to proceed. She might have management experience, but she'd never run a beach resort before. And now with Michele gone, the woman's experience was gone, as well.

But before she could pick up the phone and call the former assistant manager, and pick her brain, a man with a bushy beard and a sort of ruffled, unkempt look walked into her office—without knocking, she noticed.

She didn't recognize him at first, even though he looked kind of familiar.

"Yes?" she said, a little annoyed. She hated when people just barged into her office.

"You don't remember me, do you?" said the man, a little gruffly, she felt.

"Should I?" she asked.

"Cole Newman? I'm in charge of maintenance around here?"

She leaned back. Talk about a blast from the past. "I do remember you," she said, nodding. "You grew a beard, Cole." If that's what you could call the hideous thing.

He touched the beard and displayed what might be construed as a smile. She remembered Cole hadn't smiled a lot back then either. He was a great kisser, though. They'd spent hours practicing the fine art of canoodling, mostly on the beach, so their parents wouldn't find out, since they were deemed too young.

"So what can I do for you, Cole?" she said briskly, putting those memories firmly back in the place where they belonged: in the very distant past.

His brief smile was replaced by a disgruntled look. "Steven tells me you're the general manager now?"

"That's right. But only for the time being, until we find a replacement for Michele."

"Yeah, she told me she quit to go and work for the competition."

She gave him a bright smile. "Well, if you're worried about your future here at the resort, Cole, I can assure you that my father's passing, or Michele leaving, won't affect the way this place is being run. Your position is safe. Absolutely."

The mention of her father's death made the handyman grimace. "I'm sorry about your dad," he said. "I heard about what happened. He was a good man. Even though we hadn't seen him around all that much lately, he always tried to do the right thing by everyone here. He'll be missed."

His words touched Grace's heart. It was the first time anyone had talked about her dad in a positive light. "He will be missed," she agreed soberly. Not in the least by her. She might not always have seen eye to eye with her father, but she'd been very fond of him, and still remained fond, in spite of what had transpired. In fact she had always gotten along better with her dad than with her mom. She'd had furious rows with her mom in her teenage years. In the time since, she had mellowed a lot, and so had her mom, and all of that stuff just seemed very silly now.

When Cole didn't speak again, she raised an inquisitive

eyebrow. "Very kind of you to drop by, Cole," she said. "So if there's nothing else..."

"I was doing some repairs yesterday," the handyman announced, causing her to assume he wasn't finished yet, and she would enjoy his company for a few moments more. Not that she minded, but she did have a lot of work to do. But she decided to tamp down on her impatience—a bad habit, she knew—and hear the man out. "And I happened to overhear a conversation that gave me cause for concern."

"Yes?" she said, having no idea where Cole was going with this.

"There's this couple that have been coming here for years," he said, as he drew back a chair and planted himself on it, wide-legged, and clearly not ready to leave any time soon. "Terry and Heather Davis. They've been coming here since the place was founded by your late grandfather. And so I was fixing a tap in their bathroom yesterday when I heard them talking about some financial trouble they're in."

"Financial trouble?"

"Yeah, they seem to think they won't be able to pay their bill, and they were worried they might be kicked out if anyone found out."

"Well, Cole, I hate to remind you, but if guests can't pay their bills, they should probably leave. There's no two ways about it. We're not a charity, unfortunately. We've got our own bills to pay. Your salary, for one thing."

His expression hardened. "You've changed," he said curtly.

"What do you mean?"

"The old Grace would never have said a thing like that."

"The old Grace probably didn't understand how the world works," she countered. "She hadn't had to work for a living yet, and make rent every month."

He held up his hands in a peaceable gesture. "Okay, you're right. We all have bills to pay, and nothing is for free. But isn't there some way we could help them out? I mean, they're practically family, Grace. They've been coming here for so long people have started to consider them like the resort's good luck charm. We even have guests who time their stay with Terry and Heather's presence here. They're like part of the furniture." He winced. "That didn't sound right."

"No, but I understand," said Grace. "I think I remember Terry and Heather. Or at least I seem to remember Dad talking about them. They booked their honeymoon here, didn't they? Back when the resort first opened for business?"

"I think they were your grandfather's first guests, probably fifty years ago."

"And you're telling me they won't be able to pay for their stay with us this time?" She found herself staring at Cole's beard, and wondering why he'd ever grown it, and why he didn't bother to trim it, or tame it. It looked like some wild animal had attached itself to his face. But then the whole man looked a little wild. She didn't remember him looking like this before. He'd been just a kid, of course, but very handsome. Like a young Jeff Bridges. Now he looked like a middle-aged Jeff Bridges. Or even an old Jeff Bridges. It was the beard. A beard aged people.

"That's what I gathered," Cole confirmed. "I just thought you should know, so maybe we could do something about it. Comp their room, maybe? Or find some other way to help out?"

"I don't know, Cole." She wasn't a social worker, and she knew she wasn't good with this kind of stuff. Still, if they'd been coming here for fifty years, and had always been good customers, she didn't see why they couldn't make a gesture this one time. So she made a decision. "You know what? Why don't I go over there and have a chat with them? What room are they in, do you know?"

Cole gave her a smile now, and it was as if the sun broke

through the clouds. His grumpy face really opened up, and she could see he was still the same Cole she remembered, even if his face was now hidden underneath a thick layer of shrubbery. He gave her the room number, and added, "Can you leave me out of it, though? I don't want them to think I was spying on them or something."

"Of course," she assured him. It was really kind of him to go out of his way to do this. "Oh, and Cole," she added when he got up to leave, "nice to see you again."

The smile persisted, and even as he walked out, after giving her a sort of half-hearted salute and a grunt, she felt slightly better about taking over this position. Maybe she would be able to manage being a general manager after all.

She picked up her phone, and for the next half hour proceeded to grill Michele Bouvier about the ins and outs of her job. By the end, she had the woman agreeing to sit down with her so they could organize a decent transition.

"That's very kind of you, Michele," she said, much relieved. "Honestly I wouldn't know where to begin."

"You'll get the hang of it soon enough," said Michele. "It's not that hard." She paused. "I'm sorry I walked out on you like that—leaving you in the lurch. It's just that I've been wanting to leave for months, and when I heard your dad had died, and that some investor was taking over, I figured it was time for me to go."

"No, I get that," she said. "And I don't blame you. If the Argent offered me a job, I might accept it, too."

Michele laughed. "Yeah, right. A Wheeler working for the Argent. As if that'll ever happen."

Grace smiled. "You're right. That probably wouldn't be right." Besides, they'd probably think she was trying to spy on them. "Oh, and one more thing before I let you go. You wouldn't happen to know Terry and Heather Davis, would you?"

"Of course. They're the resort's most favorite couple. What about them?"

She told Michele about the couple's financial trouble, and Michele said the resort had a small war chest for such contingencies. "You can comp them the room," she suggested. "Pay for it from the emergency kitty. Though it surprises me that they would be having this kind of trouble. As far as I understand they own their own house, and they've got a nice nest egg squirreled away. Terry used to own his own gardening business, and Heather worked in housekeeping all her life at some small hotel in Queens or Brooklyn. They shouldn't be having financial problems. Terry sold his business a couple of years ago and Heather retired."

As Grace hung up the phone, she wondered how to handle this. She couldn't very well blurt out that she knew about the couple's lack of funds. That wouldn't go over well. So how to proceed?

And as she was thinking about this, she stepped out of the office to go in search of the couple. She passed the lobby just when a man walked in. And as their eyes met, her breath caught in her throat.

It was Jay Polys! Her old boss!

CHAPTER 20

Much to Grace's consternation, it transpired that the man who'd dumped her when their affair became public knowledge, and who'd filed an ethics complaint against her, causing her career to implode, was the mystery investor her dad had brought on board to save the Hampton Cove Resort & Spa!

She stared daggers at the man, as they all sat down for a frank discussion in one of the conference rooms. Grace's sisters were there, and so was Nicolas.

"So you're back, are you?" said Polys, a grin playing about his lips. "Who would have thought?"

"This is my family's resort," Grace snapped. "Which gives me every right to be back. What are you doing here?"

He spread his arms. "I bought the place."

Murmurs of astonishment filled the room. "You *bought* the resort?" asked Lauren. "The whole resort?"

"An eighty-percent share," said Polys smoothly.

Lauren turned to Nicolas. "You didn't mention that."

"I didn't know," Nicolas murmured, looking distinctly ill at ease. "The exact terms of the agreement were kept confidential, for obvious reasons. Only your dad and Mr. Polys were privy to that information."

"So you own the whole resort?" asked Grace, shocked by this development.

"Eighty-percent share," Polys repeated. "Which effectively makes me the majority shareholder. Your dad was facing bankruptcy, and had started looking for an investor, and so that's how I came on board."

"But why us—why *you?*" asked Grace.

"Actually it was you who gave me the idea," said Polys. "You talked about the resort so much I got curious. And so I did some research. Turns out the number-one resort on the coast here is the Argent, with the Hampton Cove a distant second. Your glory years are in the past, though, as your father was frank enough to disclose. But with some changes made, and money invested, I saw no reason why this place can't become great again—maybe even greater than the Argent."

"What changes?" asked Jill, who'd been chewing a fingernail.

"Oh, we can talk about that later," said Polys. "Right now I want to bring in a consultant to audit the books, and take a closer look at the entire operation."

"Didn't you audit the books before you made the investment?" asked Grace, who knew Polys as a skilled operator. Nothing got past the guy.

"I did, yes," he said with a smile. "This will be an even more thorough audit."

"I can't believe Dad sold the resort," said Lauren.

"Eighty percent," Polys corrected. "Your family still owns twenty percent."

"I don't get it!" Grace burst out. "You could have spent your millions anywhere, but you had to go and buy my family's business. Why, Jay, why!" Her sisters and Nicolas looked embarrassed by her outburst, but she didn't care. She had to know.

"Because it's a sound investment," said the entrepreneur with a shrug. "And because I like the business. I happen to think we could do so much more with this place. Really take it to the next level. For one thing, the corporate market is huge, and yet the Hampton Cove hasn't tapped it. Not to the extent that it could. Why? We could organize company retreats. Rent out these conference rooms so companies can organize their meetings here. That's where the money is. And when all is said and done, I want to take this concept and turn it into a franchise." He got a sort of dreamy look about him that Grace knew all too well. He was dreaming big—bigger than big. He was dreaming global. "Can you imagine Hampton Cove resorts on every coast and in every country around the world? This is a concept that will travel. And we're the ones who'll take it there."

"I don't want this concept to travel," said Grace acidly. "I just want to run my family's resort the way it's always been run: by making it a great place for families, where they can relax and have a wonderful, relaxing time."

"That's exactly what I want!" said Polys, jumping up and pacing the room. He abruptly turned. "I have a feeling we're going to work well together, Grace."

"And I don't," she said. "In fact I'm going to ask you to leave now."

He laughed. "I could ask you the same thing." He leaned in, and a threatening note crept into his voice. "I'm your boss now, Grace. Whether you like it or not."

"And see how well that turned out the last time," she said, meeting his gaze.

His killer smile faltered. "Yeah, well, I had no choice. The takeover was on the line. If I hadn't filed that complaint against you, the investor would have walked. And as founder and president I had an obligation to my shareholders."

"The company would have been just fine," said Grace. "But you wouldn't have had your big payday. And that's all that mattered to you. That's why you filed that ethics complaint, even though you knew full well that was a big, fat lie. And that you were destroying my career."

He gave her a breezy look. "You seem to have done okay for yourself."

"Oh, just leave," she said, utterly sick of the man. "Just go."

"I can see you're upset, so I'm going to give you a moment to compose yourself," said Polys. "But I'll be back, and if I find that we can't work together in a day-to-day capacity, I'm sorry to say you're the one who'll have to leave, Grace."

And with these words, he strode out of the conference room.

"And stay gone!" she yelled at his retreating back.

For a moment, an electric silence hung in the room, then Nicolas said, "Looks like this new investor isn't as silent as your dad said he was going to be."

"No, looks like he wants to be very hands-on," said Lauren.

"Jay is always hands-on," Grace said, tapping the table. "He's a hands-on kind of guy." And when she saw that all those present were eyeing her with a touch of astonishment, mixed with amusement, she added, "Don't look at me like that."

"So now what?" asked Lauren finally.

"I'm telling you, if he stays, I go," said Grace.

"You can't go, honey," said Lauren. "This is our family's business."

"Not anymore, it's not," said Grace.

"Yeah, looks like Dad sold it out from under us," Jill added.

"Can he do that?" asked Lauren. "Can he sell this place without Mom's signature?" Her question was directed at Nicolas, who looked as puzzled and surprised as they all were.

"I think we probably need to speak to a lawyer," said Grace. "And figure out what's going on here. A silent investor who says he'll be here to handle day-to-day operations. The owner's husband who sells the business without the actual owner's approval. Something is fishy here." And she meant what she'd said: if Polys stuck around, she was gone, even if it meant giving up her family's business.

"We'll figure it out," said Lauren, always the most sensible one. "We have to."

* * *

STEVEN AND HAZEL had seen Jay Polys leave the conference room and stalk across the lobby like a caged tiger, his eyes shooting flames while tying his suit jacket and straightening his tie, and wondered what was going on.

"He looks like a shark," said Hazel. "Like one of them corporate raiders."

"Jay Polys," said Steven.

"Polys as in Polys Cars?"

"That's the one. Though he sold the company, and became a billionaire in the process. So if my gut isn't misleading me, I think we've just seen the new boss."

"He's the investor Michele was talking about?"

Steven nodded seriously. "And judging from all the screaming and shouting just now, I think it's safe to say his arrival wasn't greeted with cheers and applause." He turned to Hazel, lowering his voice. "And I think I know why that might be. Grace used to work for that guy. And rumor has it they were having an affair. This was before she was fired, though, following an ethics complaint he filed against her."

"How do you know all this?" asked Hazel, who was usually the one spreading all the gossip.

"I've got my sources," said Steven. When Hazel gave him a look, he took out his phone. "And I can read the business press," he added, and pulled up the article in the Wall Street Journal where it was reported that Grace Wheeler had been fired as vice president of Polys, the well-known ride-sharing company, following an ethics complaint filed against her by founder, CEO and president Jay Polys himself. And even though the contents of the complaint were confidential, the paper had spoken to two people who were familiar with the circumstances of Miss Wheeler's shocking dismissal, and said they were in the nature of a MeToo affair.

"So she was having an affair with him," said Hazel, quickly scanning the article.

"It's entirely possible his wife found out, and so he filed the complaint against Grace, hoping to save his marriage. Or she could have been harassing him, and he finally had enough."

"Not Grace," said Hazel. "She would never do something like that."

Steven took his phone and gave his colleague a meaningful look. "That's what people said about Johnny Wheeler. And look what he did."

"He wasn't exactly harassing Juda Andrews, though, was he?"

"No," said Steven, raising a sardonic eyebrow. "Mrs. Andrews clearly enjoyed the treatment. At least I never heard any complaints from her."

CHAPTER 21

Nicolas had walked out of the meeting feeling a little lightheaded. Meetings often had that effect on him, but today was different. All this screaming and shouting wasn't good for his equanimity. And also, it wasn't what he was used to in his job. Nobody ever shouted in the presence of the accountant. Mostly people treated him with the utmost respect. Sometimes they got a little bored, and sometimes they almost fell asleep. But there was never any drama. And now this. Maybe he should have followed Michele's advice and quit his job? A good accountant could always find another. And frankly if this was the way things were going to be from now on, he could think of better ways to spend his time.

Steven and Hazel beckoned him over, and so he proceeded to give them a blow-by-blow account of what had transpired in the meeting. He could see from their shiny eyes that his story didn't disappoint. In fact it was probably even more shocking than what their combined imaginations had already concocted.

"Oh, my God," said Steven, clutching a distraught hand to

his face. "Next thing you know they'll get physical and actually start slugging it out."

"I doubt it," said Hazel.

"Yeah, Polys doesn't look like the kind of man who'd pick a fight," said Steven, and there was a touch of wistfulness in his eyes. "Still, a boy can dream."

"What are you talking about?" said Hazel. "Don't you see this could be the end of the Hampton Cove? What if the Wheeler sisters decide to jump ship, and we're left at the mercy of this billionaire? Do you know what will happen to this place?"

"We'll all get a pay raise and a snazzy new outfit?" Steven suggested.

"This place will turn into one of those cookie-cutter resorts, like you can find in any town in any country around the world. And we'll be replaced by younger models, more handsome, who'll have to work twice as hard for half the pay."

"I doubt they'll be able to find anyone who's more handsome than me," Steven murmured.

"This has always been a family-run business," Hazel continued. "Which is exactly why I like it here. Okay, so it's not exactly a high-end resort, but it's got a great atmosphere, casual and comfortable, and that's why a lot of our guests are regulars, and keep coming back year after year. Heck, we've got people who first came here as kids, and now they've got kids of their own. And at some point their kids will have kids, and they'll all come and stay at the Hampton Cove. Because that's how much they love it here."

"It's true," said Nicolas. "The Argent may offer a better experience, but the Hampton Cove has that family vibe—a wonderful ambiance, hands down."

"So you're telling us this Polys guy now owns the place?" asked Hazel.

"Johnny sold him an eighty-percent stake in the business," Nicolas confirmed.

"God, what an idiot," said Hazel, shaking her head. "What a fool."

"In all fairness, I don't think Johnny knew he was selling the place to his daughter's now ex-boyfriend," said Nicolas. And when two pairs of eyes drilled into his, he told them about the affair. They already seemed to know all about it, though, which was to be expected. Hazel and Steven were the masters of gossip.

The accountant watched on as Steven seemed momentarily distracted.

"What's wrong?" he asked.

Steven was fumbling with a small note, his face having paled.

"Steven has a secret admirer," Hazel revealed.

"A stalker, more like," said the receptionist. He showed them the little note he'd received. There were hearts and flowers surrounding a small love poem.

"It's cute," said Nicolas.

"I don't know," said Steven. "It's making me nervous."

"Why?"

"Because it's probably from one of the guests, only I don't know which one!"

"He'll reveal himself to you sooner or later," Hazel assured their friend and colleague. "When the time is right, he'll come right out and show his face."

Steven chewed his lip. "But what if I don't like him? I hate this whole buildup. Why can't he just do like normal people, and find me on Grindr?"

Nicolas uttered a startled laugh, but when Steven continued to look distressed, he said, "Just ignore it for now would be my advice. And if he does pop out of the woodwork at some point, you'll know if you like him or not, and you can decide then and there if you want to go out with him."

"Or her," said Steven. "It could be a woman." He looked absolutely horrified by this prospect, however slim the chance might be. One look at Steven Lesinske was enough to convince anyone he wasn't into the members of the female persuasion.

"I'm sure it's a he," said Hazel, patting the receptionist's back.

"I hope so," said Steven, clutching at his throat. "This day just keeps getting more and more interesting. Between Mr. Billionaire becoming our new boss, and my stalker, I'm starting to think Michele pulled the trigger too soon."

"What do you mean?" asked Nicolas.

Steven shrugged. "Michele left to go and work for the Argent, but now this place is turning into a second Argent, so she could just have stuck around instead."

"I don't like it," Hazel muttered, as she took her leave. "I don't like this at all."

"What do you think about all of this, Nicolas?" asked Steven.

"I think I'll reserve judgment until I know more about the new boss's plans."

"Spoken like a true accountant," said Steven with an expressive eye roll.

CHAPTER 22

Bea paused in the driveway. She had more or less made up her mind to leave the house for the first time since Johnny died, but now that she was actually having to get into the car and drive into town, she was having second thoughts. The undertaker had called, and asked to meet so they could arrange the details for the funeral. She could have told him to come to the house, but that just seemed silly. She wasn't an invalid, and she hadn't lost her mind. She could drop by his office and handle the matter face to face. In fact the sooner it was over the better.

One thing she wasn't going to change her mind about was her presence at the funeral. After Johnny's betrayal—his multiple betrayals—the last thing she wanted was to honor her husband's passing by attending the man's funeral. He didn't deserve it, and she wasn't prepared to allow the whole town to watch as she collapsed under the pressure. Which she was quite sure was what would happen if she went. The entire town would come out—that was a given. But she wouldn't give them the satisfaction. Or Juda—especially Juda.

She thought for a moment, her hand on the black Range Rover for support. Her heart was beating a mile a minute, which was just ridiculous. She hadn't done anything wrong. She wasn't a war criminal, for crying out loud. Her husband had cheated on her, and had neglected the business her father had entrusted to him. That was on him, not her. So why should she feel nervous about facing people?

Finally she pulled herself together and got into the car. She knew that if she didn't do this now, she might never leave the house again. And in spite of her impassioned little speech to her kids, and the grand fantasy of relocating to Belize or Mexico, she knew that she wasn't going to do that —ever. She wasn't going to let anyone drive her away from her home and her family. Instead she was going to live her life, whatever anyone else might think about her.

The visit to the funeral parlor actually went a lot better than she had expected. And once the funeral arrangements were taken care of, she had to admit she was feeling much relieved. She hadn't realized how much she was dreading the prospect of having to deal with the details of her husband's sudden death. Now that that was all behind her, she could finally start looking forward, instead of back.

And she was walking back to the car when a cry of surprise had her look up. She wasn't pleased when she saw it was Ruth Gaynor, one of her so-called best friends, making a beeline for her. Ruth was clutching a brand-new Louis Vuitton bag in her hand, and had clearly been enjoying her favorite hobby: retail therapy.

"Oh, my God, Bea!" Ruth was crying as she hurried to reach her, which took some time, as she was wearing her usual stilts again. "Am I happy to see you!"

Bea would have said the feeling wasn't mutual, but she had been raised better than that. Never one for starting a public brawl, instead she plastered a smile onto her face, and greeted her friend. "I've been meaning to call," she said, even though it wasn't true.

Ruth had always been more Juda's friend than Bea's, and so Bea was pretty convinced that Ruth had known all about Juda's betrayal, and yet had chosen to stay quiet, and allow the affair to continue behind Bea's back all these years.

"How are you?" asked Ruth. "God, such a terrible shock. How are you holding up?"

"Barely," she admitted. "It *was* a great shock. First to find Johnny in bed with Juda, and then to watch him collapse right in front of me."

"And die," Ruth stressed.

"Yes, and die," said Bea.

"Well, at least he didn't suffer," said Ruth, who was clearly grasping at straws to keep the conversation going. What do you tell a woman whose husband was sleeping with a mutual best friend?

"No, at least there's that," Bea agreed, though she wouldn't have minded if Johnny had suffered. In fact she felt he'd gotten off easy by dying on her instead of facing the music like a man.

"I heard your girls have moved back in with you?" said Ruth, eyeing her with a touch of nervousness. "That's so nice of them, to be there for you just when you need them. I wish my kids would be so considerate. Instead they can't get far enough away from us, it seems."

Bea murmured her sympathy, keeping one eye on her escape route. This wasn't the way she'd hoped her first venture into town would go. There was always the risk, of course, of running into people she knew. But she'd hoped to avoid it for as long as possible. Then again, she had to face these people sooner or later, so maybe this was the way it was supposed to be. She could just get it over with now, and not have to worry about it anymore—dreading the confrontation.

And so she decided to take the bull by the horns. "Have you seen Juda since… the incident?" she asked.

Ruth studied her for a moment, then nodded. "She's devastated. Absolutely devastated."

As she should be, Bea thought. "She's been trying to call me," she said. "But of course I refuse to talk to her."

"Oh, but I can imagine," said Ruth sympathetically, though still studying her as one would a bomb that's about to go off and you want to run for cover in case it does.

Bea took a deep breath, and looked her friend in the eye. "There's one thing I've been wondering, Ruth."

"Yes?" said Ruth, a little uncertainly.

"Did you know about Johnny and Juda?"

Ruth opened her mouth to speak, then seemed to think better of it, and finally nodded. A blush had spread across her cheeks, and she seemed to reconsider the wisdom of approaching Bea to have this little chat.

"I thought you did. You and Juda have always been close." She would have asked Ruth why she hadn't told her, but the answer was obvious. One doesn't disclose a secret affair to the woman being cheated on. It can only lead to trouble.

"I should have told you," said Ruth finally. "In fact I wanted to tell you a million times, but I'd promised Juda I wouldn't. And so, like a true coward, I kept quiet."

"It would have been nice if someone told me that my husband was seeing another woman behind my back for the past five years," Bea agreed.

"Five? Has it really been five years?"

"Five years," Bea confirmed. "Five flower shows, five Christmas parties, and countless other social engagements where the four of us were chatting as if nothing was going on —and all this time you knew. You knew and you chose to keep quiet." She shook her head. "That's not friendship, Ruth. You weren't being my friend when you did that. And neither was Juda, but that's a given, of course."

"I know," said Ruth, and she had the decency to look miserable. "But Juda made me promise, and also, she told me it wasn't going to be like this forever."

"What do you mean?"

But Ruth had turned fidgety again. "That's not for me to say."

"What's not for you to say? Ruth, for heaven's sakes, tell me."

"I can't," said Ruth. "Juda is the one who should tell you, not me."

"Well, then Juda can wait a long time, because I'm never going to talk to that woman again for as long as I live."

"You don't mean that," said Ruth, staring at her in shock.

"What did you expect? The woman betrayed me, Ruth."

"But… she's your friend. Your very best friend. She loves you."

"She's got a strange way of showing it," Bea scoffed.

"Look, talk to Juda. Things are not always what they seem," said Ruth, patting her on the arm, then thinking better of it when Bea momentarily froze. She quickly removed her hand. "Just talk to her. Let's deal with this like grown-ups."

"Oh, I am dealing with this like a grown-up. By cutting Juda from my life."

"Oh, Bea," said Ruth, shaking her head in dismay. "Have you ever considered that there are two sides to this story?"

"I don't see how there could be. From where I'm standing the story is pretty clear."

"Talk to Juda. Please. For all our sakes. And let's put this thing behind us."

"We're never going to put this behind us, Ruth. And besides: there is no more we. From now on, 'we' doesn't exist anymore. Juda destroyed that when she decided to start fooling around with my husband behind my back."

And with these words, she walked away. Ruth had quite a nerve, she thought, to insist they put this sordid affair behind them. As far as she was concerned, their friendship had suffered a terminal collapse, and could never be revived.

She got in the car, and watched as Ruth hesitated for a moment, then walked off. But not before darting a final glance in her direction. She looked sad, Bea thought, and suddenly she wondered if Ruth had also had an affair with Johnny.

There were two sides to this story, Ruth had said. Could it be that Johnny was having an affair with both women? And that Juda had cheated on Ruth as well? Or maybe Ruth's husband was also having an affair? Possibly with Juda?

Knowing what she knew now, she wouldn't it past the woman.

Her phone chimed, and when she picked it out of her purse, she saw that it was Lauren. "Hi, sweetie," she said. "How are things at the resort?"

"Mom, you have got to get over here!" said Lauren, sounding breathless.

"What do you mean? What's wrong?"

"If you want to stop a murder, you better get your ass over here now!"

CHAPTER 23

Bea parked her car in the resort parking lot and immediately saw what the problem was. Standing next to a sleek silver convertible, Grace was going toe to toe with a handsome man dressed in black, with a ponytail and a stylishly coiffed beard. She had no idea who the man was, but thought this just might be the outside investor Johnny had brought in to save the resort from ruin.

Lauren came hurrying up to her. Her middle child was biting her lip. Meanwhile, Jill was nowhere to be seen, which wasn't unusual, as her youngest hated conflict, which might be one of the reasons she'd fled to the East. Even though Bea hadn't known it at the time, Jill must have sensed that trouble was brewing in her and Johnny's marriage.

"Who's he?" asked Bea.

"Jay Polys," said Lauren. "He's the investor. But also, and more importantly, he's Grace's former boss."

"The one she had an affair with and who fired her?"

Lauren nodded. "One and the same."

"Oh, dear. This isn't good."

"You're telling me. They already came to blows inside,

and then when Polys walked out, Grace followed him out here for part two of their big dust-up."

"A lot of repressed anger," said Bea as she watched her eldest go red in the face as she gave as good as she got. It satisfied her to see that she had the billionaire cornered.

"You have to do something, Mom," said Lauren. "You're the only one Grace listens to."

"You could have fooled me," said Bea. "I doubt Grace listens to anyone these days." She used to listen to Johnny, but that was a long time ago. Grace and Johnny always had a special connection, a connection Johnny had essentially squandered.

Bea walked up to the feuding pair, and as she approached, held out her hand. "Bea Wheeler," she said. "And you must be Jay Polys. So nice to meet you."

Grace had shut up the moment her mom arrived, but her face was working, and steam was practically pouring from her ears.

"Hi, Mrs. Wheeler," said Polys, taking her hand. "I've heard so much about you."

"Only good things, I hope," she said, as she watched Grace perform the perfect eye roll. "I understand that you and Grace know each other?"

"Yes, you can say that," said Polys. "Grace used to work for me."

"Until you fired me, after destroying my career and my future."

"I told you, I had no other choice. If I hadn't done what I did, the investor would have walked, and then we wouldn't be where we are now."

"All I'm hearing is that you chose a big fat paycheck over me," said Grace, pointing a finger at the man's chest. "Which tells me everything I need to know about the kind of person you are." She turned to her mother. "Can you believe this is the guy Dad sold the resort to? Eighty percent! He now owns eighty percent of this place! Our family business—sold right from under you."

This statement, as well as the vehemence with which it was delivered, took Bea by surprise. "Johnny sold you eighty percent of the shares in the resort?"

The tech billionaire nodded. "He said he needed a quick injection of cash, and when the number crunchers had run through the numbers, eighty percent is what we came up with. Your husband made some unsound investments these past couple of years, and the resort was hemorrhaging money at an unhealthy rate. If I hadn't come on board, Johnny would have had to declare bankruptcy."

"He never told me about any of that," said Bea, stunned by this piece of news.

"You have to talk to a lawyer, Mom," said Grace. "I'm pretty sure this whole deal is illegal. Dad didn't have the right to sign the contract without your approval."

"And I can assure you that everything was above board," said Polys smoothly. "Johnny was fully authorized to take any decision necessary, including a sale."

Grace eyed her mother fiercely. "He's lying, Mom. You own the resort, not Dad."

"Well..." said Bea. "It is true that I signed a power of attorney at some point."

Grace stared at her. "Mom!" she cried finally. "How could you!"

"It's the way we worked things out early on in our marriage. Johnny was going to be in charge of the resort, taking over from my dad when he retired, and I had made it clear from the beginning that I had no interest in any of that. We were all very happy that Johnny wanted to step in. Otherwise we would have had to sell the place, and Daddy would have hated that, since he was the one who made it what it is today."

"Like I said, Johnny was perfectly within his right to take any measure necessary when it came to handling the resort's legal and business affairs," said Polys. "So the contract is valid, and I am now the majority shareholder of the Hampton Cove Resort & Spa. And since I intend to take an active role in its management, I suggest you think very carefully about your position, Grace."

"I am the general manager now," said Grace stubbornly.

"That's fine," said Polys. "As long as you don't forget I am the owner. Which means I'm your boss."

"You're not my boss, and you're not the owner," said Grace, once more bridling at this man's presumptuous attitude. "We're both co-owners."

"But since I own an eighty-percent share, I'm the majority owner, so my word goes," Polys insisted stubbornly.

"Over my dead body," said Grace, once more approaching the man, and going toe to toe with him. But Polys stood his ground, since he knew he had the law on his side, whatever Grace might say.

"Look, we don't need to argue this out in the parking lot," said Bea, who had noticed that a small crowd of people had gathered around, and they were very interested in what these two had to say. "Why don't we take this discussion inside? Before your little contretemps is all over the evening news?"

Polys glanced up, and when he saw the audience they'd drawn, he patted his shiny black hair, smoothed his ponytail, and nodded. "Let's take this inside," he agreed. "Grace?"

Grace seemed reluctant to let this go, but finally she saw the wisdom of her mother's words, and the four of them walked in the direction of the resort.

"I can't believe you're trying to fire me again," Grace hissed.

"Not here, Grace," said Bea. "We don't wash our dirty laundry in public."

"What are you doing here, anyway?" asked Grace. "I thought you said you weren't going to leave the house again —ever?"

"I called her," said Lauren. "Before you two killed each other."

"I would never kill Grace," said Polys. He grinned—a charming smirk. "At least not in public."

Once inside, they moved to the conference room, where the two antagonists sat down and the argument started all over again, only this time with Bea and Lauren as their arbiters. It soon became clear that Polys had the law on his side. He had bought the resort fair and square, and had found in Johnny the legal owner—through the power of attorney Bea had signed—to handle the sale. So technically there was nothing any of them could do about this. Johnny hadn't merely cheated on his wife by sleeping with her best friend, he'd also sold her business out from under her, after draining it of cash so he could keep his girlfriend in style: holidays in Courchevel, Monaco and St Barts, according to the girls, lots of fancy cars and even a yacht, and of course clothes and jewelry.

And when finally the resort had been bled dry, he'd sold it to Grace's former boss, an unscrupulous tech billionaire, who'd destroyed his daughter's career.

If Johnny hadn't died, she could have killed him, Bea thought as she mulled this all over. The good news was that the resort was saved, and that Polys appeared to have a genuine interest in making some much-needed investments.

"Look," said Bea finally, "if there's one thing that we all have in common, it's that we genuinely care about this place. And we want to see it prosper."

"Of course," Polys agreed. "When Grace first told me

about her family's resort, I did some research, and fell in love with the place. Which is when the idea started to form in my mind one day to own it."

"You stayed here?" asked Lauren.

"I did. And I have to say that of all the beach resorts I've ever visited, the Hampton Cove made the best impression on me. Not in terms of luxury arrangements or quality, but in terms of the heart of the place, and the people who work here as well as the guests. Your resort truly is a family resort, created by and for families, and that's what makes the difference. At least that was my experience."

"It's true," said Bea. "That's how my dad envisioned the resort, and also what Johnny tried to preserve." Until somehow he had a change of heart, and priorities.

"Look, I don't want to fight your family on this," said Polys to Grace. "Instead I want us to work together. And I know we can, since we worked together in the past, and it's the work we did that turned Polys into the juggernaut it is today."

"Until you fired me and tried to destroy my life," Grace repeated.

"That was wrong of me and I regret it now," said Polys, a rare moment of reflection for the man. "I admit that I panicked, and when our Chinese investor called me and confronted me with the story, threatening to pull out, I came up with this story, and then of course I had to follow through on the narrative, even if it cast you in the light of the villain of the story. And I'm truly sorry. I really am."

He seemed genuine enough, Bea thought, but Grace wasn't having it.

"You could have taken your responsibility, instead of feeding me to the lions."

"I know. And you're right," said Polys softly.

There was a momentary silence, as the two opponents sized each other up.

"Looks like we're forced to work together again," said Polys finally, and held out his hand. "Truce?"

But Grace wasn't taking this opportunity. Instead, she rose to her feet. "Not a chance," she said. Then eyed Polys coldly. "I guess we'll see each other in court."

And she walked out, leaving the others reeling at this denouement.

"You raised a stubborn daughter," said Polys finally as he, too, got up.

"I raised a proud daughter," said Bea. "And you have to admit she has a point."

But Polys didn't see it that way. "We're wasting valuable time. The resort is sinking fast. You've already lost your general manager and several other key people, and if the rest of the staff get word of a conflict of ownership, they'll leave the sinking ship as well, and pretty soon there will be nothing left." He gave Bea a knowing look. "For me this would be a simple write-off, a minor fraction of my fortune lost, but for you? Losing the company? The business your father built, and your husband? Maybe you better have another word with your daughter."

And on this notion, he also left the room.

"This isn't good," said Lauren, which was quite the understatement. "We need to talk to Grace. Tell her to play nice with this guy. She may not like it, but what other choice do we have?"

"You're right," said Bea. She wasn't prepared to let her family's business go down the drain because her daughter was too stubborn to see reason. She slapped the table lightly. "We better have a family meeting, honey. Now."

CHAPTER 24

Grace had returned to her office—though apparently it was Polys's office now—where moments later her mom found her.

"We need to talk about this," said Mom.

"I know," said Grace, sinking into her chair. She was exhausted. The adrenaline that had coursed through her veins and had carried her through the confrontation with her former lover and boss was gone, and she felt wiped out.

"Look, I know that what Polys did to you was awful—unconscionable. But we also have the resort to think about," Mom reasoned as she took a seat in front of her. "Polys just told me he's prepared to walk away. To consider his purchase of the resort a write-off."

"Good," said Grace. "The sooner we get rid of that jerk, the better."

"You do realize we'll be broke if he walks."

"No, we won't. I know Polys. He'll want to unload his stake to some other investor. He doesn't care about us or this place. All he cares about is making money. Trust me, Mom. If we can raise enough money to make him an offer, he'll take it."

"But how are we going to raise that kind of money? It can't be done."

"It can be done. We'll do it. We could get a mortgage on the house, and we can pool all of our resources, and you can talk to your friends at the bank..."

"Open your eyes, Grace. Even if I mortgage the house, we'll never be able to raise that kind of money. And besides, have you seen the state of this place? The paint is peeling, the sauna and the jacuzzi look like they were built in the seventies—which they were. The pool is leaking, the rooms are old and not up to modern standards... We need Polys and his unlimited funds to turn this place around."

"I'd rather kill myself than have to work under that man again," said Grace. "You know what he did to me, Mom. He's evil."

"I don't think he's evil, honey," said Mom. "I think he made a wrong decision—a decision he now regrets, and buying this resort just may be his way of trying to make up for it."

She stared at her mother. "What do you mean?"

"Hasn't it occurred to you that that man could be doing anything right now? He could be flying to the moon, or sailing off on the biggest yacht money can buy. He could be investing in golf courses, or the latest high-tech gadget. But of all the things he could do with his money, he chose to invest in some obscure beach resort in the middle of nowhere. Some old, dilapidated family resort that by all rights should have gone under years ago through mismanagement and neglect." She touched her chest. "For which I'm partly to blame, I admit. I shouldn't have trusted your father to the extent that I did, and when I heard the stories about neglect, I shouldn't have ignored them the way I did."

"I don't know, Mom," she said, musing about her mother's arguments. "I mean, we're not as dilapidated as all that. Our guests still seem to like it here."

"But they're showing up in lesser and lesser numbers each year."

"True," Grace admitted. The numbers were down, that was true. "But the guests we do have, often have been coming here for years. They love this place for its unique atmosphere and the level of service we have to offer."

Mom gave her a kindly look. "I know you and Polys shared this terrible experience."

"We didn't share anything, Mom. He made it happen. It was his choice."

"I know. But for the sake of the resort, can't you find a way to cooperate? He's not going away, honey. And if he does, we're sunk. There's no two ways about it."

She turned in her swivel chair as she thought about this. "I refuse to answer to the man. Can you imagine him ordering me about in my own place? It's grotesque."

"I know, and I understand, which is why I'd suggest you both share the title of general manager. I know he might not agree, since technically he's got the bigger chunk of shares, but if he does, it could be the best way forward. Equal responsibility, and equal say. Of course that would mean you'd have to sit down with him, and come to some kind of arrangement. And not just one time, but on a daily basis."

Grace was already shaking her head. "If that's how it will be, I quit," she said.

"Oh, honey. But you can't quit. There's no one else right now."

"There's Polys," she pointed out. "He wants to run the show? Well, let him."

"Polys has no experience running a resort."

"Neither do I."

"No, but at least you know this place. He doesn't." Her mother got up. "Just think about it." She fixed her with a look of compassion. "Sometimes we have to swallow our pride, honey. And trust me, I know how hard it is. But if we want this place to survive, it's the only way."

And then she was gone, giving Grace a lot of food for thought indeed.

It was true that Polys, in spite of his arrogance, and his insufferable attitude, was a leader, and someone with a lot of great ideas, who brought a lot of talent to the table. With him at the helm, this place had a chance to survive, even to thrive. Without him, it might go under—which was the most likely scenario.

Did she want that? Did she want her pride to stand in the way of the resort to continue to exist? Rationally, it wasn't a tough decision to make, but emotionally it was hard—even impossible. And as she pondered the pros and cons of her mother's proposal, she finally understood that there was only one course of action open to her. And as she came to a decision, she suddenly remembered something. Terry and Heather Davis! She'd totally forgotten about the couple!

CHAPTER 25

Terry and Heather weren't to be found in their room, though. The couple were walking along the beach, and enjoying the warmth of the sun on their skin, their feet in the cooling surf. They'd spent part of the night staying up and trying to come to terms with a decision they'd more or less made the night before.

"We had a good life, didn't we?" said Terry as a wave gently splashed across his bare feet.

"We did," Heather said. "The best."

The only regret she had, and one that had haunted her for a long time, was the fact that they never had kids. When they got married, she'd dreamed of raising a big family, and when that didn't materialize, she had at first blamed Terry, then herself, when medical science had given her reason to suspect it might be her, and finally the universe, for not granting her this heart's desire. They'd tried to adopt for a while, but unfortunately hadn't been in a position to be eligible, mostly financially, while Terry was trying to build his business. It had taken long years of financial hardship before they managed to get their heads above the water and had been able to buy the house, and by then they both felt they were too old to adopt. And so gradually the acceptance had grown that they'd never have kids.

At least she had nieces and nephews, and so did Terry. All grown up by now, with kids of their own, they weren't as close as they would have liked. Most of the family had spread out across the country and abroad, and when they did speak, it was via Skype or their phones. Hard to maintain the same kind of connection as when talking in person, face to face. But that was probably the way of the times.

Heather clung to her husband's arm. It had just been the two of them these last couple of years. And frankly they didn't need anyone else. The thought had sometimes popped into her head what she'd do if Terry passed away and she found herself alone. But then he'd assured her that if their time came, they'd go together. And there was some comfort in that.

She had never been this morbid, but the older she got, the more time she spent on thoughts of their shortening future, and when this evil man had stolen their money, and their house, he'd effectively stolen what was left of their lives.

"We had a happy life," Heather now reiterated. "We were happy, weren't we?"

"The best thing that could ever have happened to me was meeting you," said Terry. "And since then, every moment spent together has been a happy moment."

It might be too much to say that every moment had been a happy moment, but Terry was right that there had been many happy moments—many happy memories. And so maybe it was time to end on a high note, just like they had agreed. To end this on their own terms, without the humiliation that was sure to come if they kept going.

And so she clutched his arm. "We'll have one final adventure," she said as she watched two kids jump in the waves and scream with joy. "One final memory."

"And we'll be together until the end, just like we promised," he said.

She smiled, and he returned her smile and pecked a gentle kiss on her lips.

"It'll be our grandest adventure ever," she whispered. "The best one yet."

* * *

Olivia was sunning by the pool, and experiencing that wonderful drowsy feeling one gets from lying in the sun—complete relaxation. Or at least partly so. Her mind kept turning over the performance from last night, when she'd sung with such abandon in front of a small crowd of resort guests. The band had asked if she was interested in doing another show tonight, and she'd already said yes.

Now she wondered if she'd allowed her post-show excitement to get in the way of her better judgment. What good could possibly come from fronting some unknown band? But then it had felt so good to finally sing again, and so maybe that was all that mattered.

And she'd just closed her eyes when a shadow drifted in front of the sun. When she looked up, she saw a man standing over her, looking down at her.

She couldn't see his face, but he was blocking out the sun.

"Could you please move?" she asked when he didn't make any attempt to. "You're blocking the sun."

The man did as he was told, but instead of removing himself from the scene, he occupied the next lounge chair, and sat down. And it was then that she recognized him. It was Diedrich Brown, legal advisor to Pastor Dean, founder and senior pastor of the OceanPeak Church. A chill immediately settled around her heart, in spite of the heat of the sun beating down on them.

The legal beagle was dressed in a suit, and looking entirely out of place.

"How did you find me?" was all Olivia asked, for it was immediately clear to her this man had come here looking for her.

"It wasn't easy," Diedrich admitted. "Until we saw a video of your performance last night on YouTube. Great show, by the way. I really enjoyed it."

She remembered now that a cameraman had been present last night, filming the show as part of a documentary the band was making. They were trying to raise their profile, and get the word out about Due Course. She should have known this would lead to trouble—but hadn't expected the repercussions to happen so fast.

"What do you want from me?" she asked.

The lawyer took out an attaché case, opened it, and extracted a document. "We want you to sign this, Olivia. Failure to do so will open you up to all kinds of legal problems. So my advice would be to sign—and sign right now."

"What is it?" she asked, though she had a good idea what it might be.

"A nondisclosure agreement. Basically it says you agree to keep anything you learned during your tenure at OceanPeak to yourself, not divulge it to anyone."

"I already told Dean I'm not signing that," she said.

"Yeah, I know. But what Senior Pastor Dean probably failed to mention is the legal position this puts you in." He leaned forward and fixed her with a serious look. "The church is a powerful institution, Olivia. And you're just one person. You can see the issue."

"I'm still not signing anything. Pastor Frank attacked me.

He should own up to what he did, instead of trying to silence me."

"We're dealing with Frank in our way," said Diedrich. "And rest assured, he won't get away with this."

"I believe he already has. He's still a pastor, isn't he? He hasn't been punished."

The man seemed annoyed by her reluctance to get this over with quickly. "Pastor Frank made a transgression, and that was wrong of him. He succumbed to the temptations of the flesh, and we're all praying with him, and he's atoning for his sins. But should the whole church be punished for one man's sin? Should his parishioners be denied access to the unique gift that Pastor Frank has? The man is blessed, Olivia. And the church is blessed to have him. And so we would like for you to sign this and return to the fold." He gave her a keen look. "We all miss you. You also have a gift. A gift God gave you. And you're denying people your gift."

"I don't deny anyone my gift. All I'm asking is that Frank be punished for what he did to me, and instead I got removed from OceanPeak One, and cast out."

"Nobody cast you out, Olivia. You cast yourself out when you refused to sign this NDA, and you threatened to take this matter public and talk to the press. You can see how we can't allow you to do that, can't you? It would destroy Frank, and it would damage the reputation of the church. But Dean has decided to give you a second chance. So sign the document, and come back. All will be forgiven. I promise." He gave her an enticing smile as he held out the document.

She glanced down at the document, then at the smarmy lawyer. "And what about Frank? Will he be removed from his position? Cause I know for a fact that he's done this before to other women. And he'll keep doing it if he's not stopped."

"Frank is a married man. He loves his wife and he loves his family. He won't do it again, I promise you," said the lawyer. But when Olivia just shook her head, he sighed, and finally put the document away again. "It's your choice. A bad choice, if you ask me, but still your choice." He closed the attaché case and looked up. "Think about it. And when you decide to do the right thing, give me a call." He handed her a card. "But don't think too long. This offer won't last forever."

"How long do I have?"

The lawyer's response was swift. "Forty-eight hours. After that, there's nothing more I can do for you. You'll be out and you'll stay out. Forever. And you know what that means."

And with these words, he rose from the lounge chair and was gone.

Olivia stared after him, and tried to still her beating heart. The presence of the lawyer, and his words, had caused her heart rate to spike. Her hands were trembling as she picked up her tube of sunscreen and started applying the cream with slow, deliberate movements, trying to get her breathing under control.

He had threatened her, she now realized, when he said she'd be cast out. It meant she would never see any of the people still in the church again. Which also meant she might never see her family again—her mom and dad, who would be told not to talk to her, since she was now officially excommunicated, and talking to her would constitute a sin.

Unless they refused, of course. In which case they'd be cast out as well.

She noticed her arms were covered in goosebumps. And that on such a warm day. And to think she'd once considered the OceanPeak Church a safe place—a place of warmth and love and kindness. Who knew it also had a cold, hard side? And that it consisted of people like Pastor Frank, who were allowed to target women with impunity?

No, she was never going back, but she might sign that

NDA. Just so she could still talk to her mom and dad. To leave the church was her decision, but it didn't have to affect her parents.

Yes, that was what she would do. She'd sign, and then she could finally put this nightmare behind her. And hopefully they'd leave her in peace.

CHAPTER 26

Tim was in his room, enjoying a lie-down after spending the morning in the sauna and jacuzzi. He felt more relaxed now than he had in a long time. He'd enjoyed a great massage, and had already booked another one for tomorrow. In fact he felt in such an uplifted mood that when his agent called, he immediately picked up.

After some back-and-forth about the Monchhichi movie, about which he said he hadn't made a decision yet, he launched into an impassioned plea for the indie movie he wanted to make, courtesy of the producer he'd met the night before.

"You can't do it, Timmy," said Steve immediately. "You just can't."

"What do you mean, I can't do it? Of course I can."

"No, you can't. How much are they going to pay you? Peanuts, right?"

"Well, we haven't actually discussed the terms of—"

"Peanuts. Cause that's all these people can afford. Or maybe you'll even throw in a freebie. Nada. Bupkis. How is that going to look to the studios wanting to hire you for their next hundred-million-dollar blockbuster, do you think? Not too good, Timmy. I'll ask them our usual quote, and they'll come right back to me with this freebie you did, and telling me your price has gone down, and they'd be right."

"It's not the same thing and you know it."

"No, but it is. It is to them. They'll figure you've decided to engage in an act of self-sabotage, and instead of offering you twenty, they'll offer you ten, or less. Or maybe they'll simply exclude you from the picture altogether, figuring that you're not an A-lister anymore, but the kind of actor who likes to do freebies for his friends. In which case they'll tap some other actor for the lead from now on."

"Look, Steve, I didn't want to have this discussion now, but I've been thinking about this for a long time, and maybe it's better to have it out into the open once and for all. I don't feel comfortable doing these big movies. These tent-pole movies. I never signed up for this kind of life. I wanted to be an actor, not a celebrity. And frankly it's all becoming a bit much for me, you know?"

"No, I don't know," said Steve. "What I do know is that you're about to throw away your career, just because you're burned out. Is that what you want?"

"I want to be an actor. Not a circus attraction."

"Be careful, Timmy, or you just might get your wish. You seem to forget that it's not easy to get where you are. A lot of people dream of the kind of success you're seeing right now. In fact thousands are waiting to take your place."

"Well, let them. Just so I can have a normal life again."

Steve sighed. "You don't seem to get it, kid. So I'll say it again. This is a once-in-a-lifetime opportunity you got right now. It won't last. It never lasts. And once you're done, you can make all the crappy movies you want. But you've got to strike the iron while it's hot. Make the most of it while you can. Cause it will be over at some point. It might be three years from now, or five, or ten, but I can guarantee you this: at some point in the future you won't be raking in this kind of dough. And you might not believe me, but there will come a time when nobody will know who you are. You'll be just another faded star, and there will be some new kid on the block who's got the looks, and who's got the talent, and he'll be the one on the cover of all the magazines, while you'll be in the back, in the 'Whatever happened to...' column." And with these words, the agent disconnected the call.

Tim stared at his phone. It was the first time Steve had hung up on him like this. Usually he couldn't stop the agent from talking his ear off.

He'd certainly given him something to think about. But the more he did, the more convinced he became that the kind of life he was leading right now wasn't for him. He really did want to make the small, independent productions, and act on the stage, and generally be the person he'd set out to be, all those many years ago. Before all the craziness started, and he'd ceased to be in charge of his life.

And as he lay back on the bed, he gave himself up to thought. He had to admit there was something in what his agent had said. On the other hand, wasn't it possible that he'd exaggerated, trying to scare him from making a career-changing decision? Steve got a nice commission for every deal he made for Tim, and that was a nice chunk of change he would have to do without if Tim persisted.

He still wasn't convinced he couldn't have the best of both worlds: make these big movies, and also make the smaller ones. There just had to be a way.

* * *

GRACE WANDERED INTO THE LOBBY, and found herself wending her way into Hazel Heflin's lair. The woman in charge of the bookings was seated at her desk, clutching a phone under her chin, talking a mile a minute. When Grace appeared at the door, she held up a finger, and gestured to a chair in front of her desk.

Grace dutifully took the suggestion and sat down. She didn't know what she was doing there, exactly, but telling herself that she was trying to get to know the place, and meeting every person under her command, even though she had already decided that she was going to relinquish that command, and cede to her former boyfriend, who could do with the place what he wanted for all she cared.

Hazel finally ended the call, and studied her for a moment. "You look tired," she concluded, with customary bluntness. "And I'm guessing that scene in the parking lot had something to do with that."

"Oh, you heard about that, did you?"

"Honey, everyone has heard about that, including half the guests."

"I shouldn't have allowed myself to get carried away like that," she said as she glanced around. The office was cozily appointed, with many pictures of families and kids, not all of them Hazel's, she assumed. "Yours?" she asked therefore.

"Oh, no," said Hazel. "I don't have kids. No, these are all guests who stayed here at some point, and who were so kind to send me letters and cards and emails telling me how happy they were to have found this place."

"I remember spending time here as a kid," said Grace with a smile, as she focused on three little girls playing in the pool and clearly having a great time. "Back when my grandfather was still running the resort. We couldn't wait to get out here and spend time in the pool." She pointed to the picture. "That's us."

"I know," said Hazel. "Your dad gave me that picture, way back when."

"You've been here a long time, haven't you?" said Grace.

Hazel laughed. "If that's a polite way of saying I'm old, thank you very much."

"Oh, no. I didn't mean it like that. I just meant, you know this place inside out."

"That, I do."

"I've got a tough decision to make," Grace said, wondering why she was telling Hazel. Then again, the woman was so easy to talk to. She reminded her of her grandmother, actually. A woman she had also often confided in. When she couldn't talk to her mom, because she was being unreasonable again, she'd talked to her grandmother instead, who'd always been kind and understanding. And so she proceeded to lay out the facts as they now appeared to be. The sale of the resort to Polys, the notion of staying on or leaving, Polys being their last hope.

"I think your mom is right," said Hazel finally, after listening carefully. "You don't want your pride to stand in the way of this place having a future."

"But if I leave, this place will still have a future," she said.

"No, it won't. The only reason Polys bought the resort is because of you. Take yourself out of the picture, and he's bound to lose interest. He might spruce it up a little, with the help of some company specializing in making an old and tired resort like ours look sparkling new again, and then sell it for a nice profit to some big international chain, who'll tear the whole place down, and build an exact replica of the hundreds of other beach resorts they've already got in their portfolio in its place. The upshot will be that we'll all lose our jobs, and the Hampton Cove Resort & Spa will lose its soul. Is that what you want?"

Grace blinked. "You don't pull any punches, do you?"

"Never have, never will," the booking agent confirmed.

"I guess in a sense I had forgotten about the resort these last couple of years."

"And look what happened: the place is a mess. And that's because you stopped caring. You and your sisters and your mom. Your whole family, in fact."

"I wonder why," Grace mused. "I used to love coming here. We had our birthday parties here, spent all summer in the pool and on the beach."

"You moved away, and so did your sisters. And we all know that out of sight is out of mind. But we never stopped offering the same service to our guests, only as the years went by, and Johnny lost interest, we got tired, and the place looks it."

"It does look tired," Grace said.

"So now you're at a crossroads, hun. Either you can walk away again, and let this place die. Or you can overcome your differences with Polys and work together to put us on top again. It's your choice."

"I know," said Grace, who had already made her choice, but was now starting to waver. She frowned. "So you really think this place is in danger of being sold?"

"Not a doubt in my mind. The moment you're gone, Polys will pull out, and that's it for us. Game over. Finished. Kaput. But it's your decision, not mine."

She blew out a sigh. "You're not making it any easier for me, Hazel."

Hazel smiled. "I should hope not. This place is my life. Take it away, and that'll be the end of me, too."

Talk about a wake-up call, Grace thought. Hazel took the picture of the three girls off her wall, which had been put up there with Blu Tack, and handed it to her. "Before you make your final decision, take some time to study this picture, and remember the good times you spent here. Go on, take it."

She took the picture, and thanked the resort's aged

booker. "Thanks, Hazel," she said. "You've given me a lot to think about."

"I trust you'll do the right thing," said Hazel.

If only she knew what the right thing was. Though chatting with Hazel had definitely put things in perspective, that much was obvious.

CHAPTER 27

The moment Grace had left, Steven dropped by. Hazel gave him a curious look. "Now what?" she said. It seemed to her that this place hadn't been this rocking for years. And now, all of a sudden, things were happening at such a frantic pace she could hardly keep up!

"I got another letter!" the receptionist cried, and dropped a small piece of paper on her desk.

"That's not a letter," she said as she eyed the thing. "That's a post-it."

"Read it," said Steven, who was too excited to stand still, and was hopping from one leg to the other, his hands clutched in front of him.

"Stop hopping as if you need to pee," she grumbled. "You're making me nervous."

"I do need to pee," said Steven. "But I wanted to show you this first."

She raised a critical eyebrow. "It's not healthy to hold your pee. It's bad for your bladder."

"Stop yapping and just read it, will you!"

And so she read it. There were more hearts and flowers,

and the message, 'Every time I see you, my heart is all aflutter. All I want is to be with you, because you turn my mind to butter.' She frowned. "This is even worse than the others. Written by a child, most likely. I mean, how can a mind turn to butter? It's physically impossible, and not very romantic, if you ask me."

"Oh, I do think it's romantic—very romantic." He gave her a fervent look. "Nobody has ever written something like that to me, Hazel. No one!"

"And nor they should. It's terrible. Poetry of the worst kind. Minds turning to butter, hearts that are all aflutter. If I were you I'd go to the cops and report this."

"I just wish he'd come forward."

"Or she."

"I think it's a he. Has to be." His eyes widened. "That rhymed!"

"Badly," she said, eyeing her friend and colleague closely.

"Who is it, Hazel? I have to know!"

"Don't look at me," she said. "I have no idea."

"But you have to know—you always know everything!"

"Not this time. You have a secret admirer, my friend, and hopefully for you he'll reveal himself sooner or later. Or maybe not, judging from these terrible poems."

"I'm just dying to find out," said Steven as he hopped to his other leg again.

"You're also dying to go to the bathroom. And you better make it quick, before you leave a puddle on my floor. Go on, get out of here, you fool!"

"A lovesick fool!" Steven cried, but did as he was told and skedaddled.

She watched him leave and shook her head. But the smile on her face was unmistakable. She loved this.

And she'd just picked up her phone again, when Nicolas walked in.

"What's going on here!" she cried, throwing up her hands in dismay. "This place is turning into Grand Central Terminal! Now what do you want?"

"How did he react?" asked Nicolas anxiously. "What did he think?"

"He thought that minds can't possibly turn to butter," said Hazel, leaning back, "and hearts going aflutter is just about the worst bilge ever put on paper. But apart from that, he was pretty excited."

"He was?" said Nicolas, and carefully lowered himself into the chair. "Oh, what do you think, Hazel? How long should I keep this up before I reveal the truth?"

"To tell you the truth, not very long. Sooner or later you'll have to come clean."

"I know," said the soft-spoken accountant. "It's just that..." He glanced down at his well-manicured hands. "I'm scared."

"What are you scared of? Either he'll be thrilled, or he'll turn you down."

"Yes, but what if he turns me down? We still have to work together. It's going to makes things very awkward between us."

"Not necessarily," said Hazel with a straight face, even though the kid was absolutely right, of course. Knowing Steven, and the kind of drama queen he was, if this affair turned nasty, the atmosphere could become decidedly frosty. Polar. But she wasn't going to tell Nicolas that. A romantic soul at heart, she was going to endorse this affair, and give it a nice big push toward the inevitable conclusion. After all, she loved both her colleagues, and figured they deserved their happiness.

"So you're advising me to do... to do what, exactly?"

"I'm advising you to tell Steven what's going on and quit butchering poetry!"

"I probably should have googled a nice poem," Nicolas

conceded. "I just wanted to write something unique, you know. Original. Straight from the heart."

"And you certainly did," said Hazel with a touch of acerbity.

Nicolas got up again. "So what do I do now?" He stood wringing his hands. "Send him another message? Or connect on Grindr, like he asked?"

"Just tell him already," said Hazel. "Stop playing games and come right out and tell him how you feel would be my advice."

"Tell him how I feel," said Nicolas, studying the wall behind Hazel as he tried to picture how the scene might play out where he declared his everlasting devotion to the amiable receptionist. "Yes, maybe you're right. So..." He waved his hands nervously. "Should I buy him flowers? A ring? Or book a brass band?"

"For the love of all that's good and holy, no brass bands, please! Nothing good ever came from involving a brass band. Just ask him out! How hard can it be?"

Nicolas gave her a reproachful look. "You're not very romantic, are you?"

"I never said I was, sweetie. Now get lost, will you? I've got work to do."

CHAPTER 28

Bea had decided to go for a quick stroll along the beach. That morning's events had upset her in a way she didn't want her daughters to know about, and she needed to think things through. She had started wondering if Johnny's behavior, and especially the cavalier way he'd neglected the resort, had originated with her. She remembered now that he once accused her of not having any interest in her family's business, and she had to admit he had a point. And if she wasn't interested herself, how could she expect him to take an interest?

She wondered now when she had stopped caring about the business her father had built. And as she took off her shoes and enjoyed the sensation of the water against her feet, she thought it might have started when her dad died, and soon after, her mom had also died. The resort reminded her of the good times they'd shared. Even as a kid, she had loved visiting her dad in his office, and goofing around. The place had only recently been built, and everything had been so exciting. And then later, when she had kids of her own, the girls had loved it just as much as she had. But that had all changed when Dad died, much too young, and everything about the resort that had been wonderful and joyful, had suddenly turned dark and sad. She simply couldn't bear to visit the place, and be reminded of those happy days.

Dad had died of heart failure, just like Johnny, and Mom had died of heart disease, though even the doctors had admitted she had probably died of a broken heart. Soon after, Grace moved away, followed by Lauren, and then finally Jill. And then at some point, Johnny's affair started. Was she to blame for all of it? Had she stopped caring about the resort, about her family, and about her marriage?

And as she gazed across the horizon, shielding her eyes, suddenly a familiar voice drew her attention. When she turned, she was surprised to see Juda.

"Bea," said her former friend, when Bea started walking away. "Bea, we need to talk about this," she insisted.

"There is nothing to talk about," she said. "I don't want to see you. Go away."

"Look, I'm sorry. I'm sorry about everything that happened. But I just want you to hear my side of the story."

"There is no 'your side' of the story," she insisted as she kept trying to remove herself from the scene. But the sand was loose, and she wasn't getting a lot of traction. At least not enough to make a dignified exit.

"Johnny told me you were getting a divorce," Juda said, and that effectively halted her in her tracks.

"What?"

"Johnny said you were going to get a divorce. Soon. He said you were sleeping in separate beds—had done for years. And that you had agreed to an amicable divorce, and he was going to marry me." She gave her a hopeless look. "I would never have gone through with this otherwise, Bea, you have to believe me. He said you were through. Your marriage was over, and you had agreed to give each other space."

She was stunned. "I never agreed to anything of the kind."

"He also said you were both free to see other people."

"Absolutely not. Nothing like that was ever talked about."

"So you're telling me he lied?"

"He did. He absolutely did."

"Oh, God," said Juda, and Bea could see she was not in a good state. She had bags under her eyes and her face was wrinkly and saggy and had a sallow complexion. She looked about a decade older. Her hair was a mess, too.

Juda sort of collapsed on the sand, her legs apparently giving out on her, and Bea reluctantly took a seat next to her. For a moment they just stared out across the ocean, then Bea said, "He really told you we were getting a divorce?"

Juda nodded. "He said you were waiting for the girls to come home for the holidays, and then you were going to tell them. And then you were going to make it official. He said your marriage had been over for a long time, but you were keeping up appearances for the sake of the girls, and for the business, of course."

"I don't understand. Why would we keep up appearances for the business?"

"He said people wouldn't come to a family resort if the family who owned it was getting divorced. He said your dad had always sold the place as a family business. And with the divorce that was all going to change."

"Johnny had been neglecting the business. He had been milking it for all he could, and then he sold it to some tech billionaire without my knowledge."

"Oh, Bea, I didn't know about that."

She frowned at her former friend. "What do you mean, you didn't know about that? He used that money to buy you expensive clothes and jewelry, didn't he? And take you on vacations to Courchevel and St Barts and Monaco."

Her former friend stared at her. "No, he didn't. Johnny

never bought me anything. Well, maybe some flowers from time to time. Oh, and he did buy me a ring. But not an expensive one."

"I don't understand. So what did he spend all that money on?"

"I don't know, Bea. I'm just telling you he didn't spend it on me."

"Is it possible he had a second girlfriend?"

"I think the most plausible answer is that he spent that money on himself. I know he kept saying that your family didn't appreciate all the sacrifices he made when he took over the running of the resort."

"He did?"

"He often told me that he felt like a prisoner, spending every waking hour running the place your dad founded. And that if he could do it all over again, he would say no when he was offered the job. He said being general manager of a resort is the kind of job that never stops. There's always something that needs to be done, some emergency that needs to be dealt with, or some new crisis."

"I know he worked hard," said Bea, feeling miserable that Johnny had never told her about the way he felt. He'd just buckled down and done the work, until he couldn't do it anymore, and then he'd simply given up, it seemed.

"He was often away for business," said Juda. "And I never asked questions."

"So many secrets," said Bea. "And so many years lost without talking to each other. If only he would have told me he was unhappy. We could have made some changes. We could have found someone to run the resort, and we could have saved our marriage."

"He often said you were hard to talk to," said Juda, giving her a sideways glance. "Though I never saw it like that. I always thought you were easy to talk to."

"Apparently not for Johnny," said Bea softly. She couldn't imagine what had gone on in her husband's head. "He trained as an engineer," she said. "And I remember that before we got married he had this burning ambition to put his mark on the world. You know, to build these amazing bridges and impressive buildings or whatever. A lasting legacy. But then I got pregnant with Grace, and so we got married, and before long, he got involved with the resort, since my dad was having some problems with his health, and I wasn't interested in taking over from him, and besides, my dad didn't think running a resort was a woman's job."

"Typical," said Juda.

"So maybe Johnny never wanted to take over the resort, but when Dad died, he felt obligated to keep running it, and shelving his own dreams. And so he started taking what he felt was owed him, and spending the money on some of the stuff he wanted, like luxury items and expensive vacations." But how had she never seen it? He kept going on these international trips, and never once had she stopped to wonder why a person running a resort is flying to Europe for some conference, or disappears for ten days for some overseas business retreat.

And somewhere along the line, Johnny had given up on their marriage as well, too busy as she was with her socialite friends and her committees and her flower shows and spring festivals to notice that her husband was deeply unhappy.

"It's my fault," she now realized. "What wife doesn't notice her husband buying himself a Ferrari or going on some expensive trip to St Barts?"

"He did mention wanting to buy himself a fancy car," said Juda. "He said he needed it for the business. That success has to be shown, and success breeds more success. I never saw the car, though. Maybe he kept it in a garage somewhere."

"Success didn't breed success, though. Instead his extreme spending almost finished off the business."

"I'm so, so sorry," said Juda. "I should have talked to you. Asked you if it was true that you were getting a divorce. But Johnny was so convincing. And he specifically told me not to tell you. And I didn't want to cause trouble, so I kept quiet until you finally made things official."

"He probably was going to divorce me," said Bea. "Which is part of why he took so much money out of the company. Like a divorce settlement before the divorce is actually pronounced. That way he already had what he wanted."

Her initial anger at Juda had dissipated. "But what about you and Jim?"

"Oh, me and Jim are ancient history," said Juda softly as she played with the sand, letting it slide through her fingers. "We're still going through the motions, but there's nothing there anymore, and we both know it. We might still keep it going for a while, or we might call it quits..." She sighed. "It's not easy to walk away from the person you built a life with. The person you have kids with. It's so much easier just to stick around, and be unhappy, than to leave and get out."

"If you're really so unhappy, it's a safe bet that Jim is also unhappy," she said. "In which case you're both miserable and maybe better off getting a divorce."

"I know," she said, still with bowed head. "I never wanted to hurt you, Bea. You're my best friend. And I can't believe..." She was tearing up, Bea saw, and actually felt for her.

She put an arm around Juda's shoulder. "Johnny should have said something. And I should have seen that he was hurting."

"And I should have ignored him and talked to you anyway. Then none of this would have happened, and maybe Johnny would still be alive."

"You miss him, don't you?"

"I do," said Juda. "I actually… liked him. A lot."

"You don't have to lie to me, Juda. You loved my husband, didn't you?"

Juda's head bobbed up and down. "I did love him," she said quietly.

God, what a mess. And now the same mess had tainted her daughters' relationships, ending them as well. Though in Jill's case that didn't seem like such a bad thing. And maybe in Lauren's case also: her husband was clearly a moron.

Juda wiped away her tears. "Can you ever forgive me?"

Bea smiled. "You know what? I think I might already have."

Which was just the strangest thing. They hugged, and Juda sniffled and even Bea shed a few tears. Johnny was gone, but at least she still had a friend left. Or maybe even more than one.

CHAPTER 29

Tim was occupying his usual spot at the far end of the bar, his ball cap pulled down low over his eyes, nursing a drink and watching the bustling activity with an amused eye. He had noticed that the resort seemed to cater mainly to families, with plenty of kids out and about, even at this relatively late hour. The parents were obviously having a ball, while the kids were also enjoying themselves.

He wondered now, not for the first time, if this kind of family life would ever be something that was in the cards for him. He'd dated off and on over the past couple of years, but it was hard to sustain a serious relationship when you were zipping across the globe all the time. Plus, not a lot of women appreciated being with a guy who was adored by millions of other women, with plenty of candidates ready and willing to throw themselves at him wherever he went.

His last serious relationship actually dated from before his career became turbocharged, and he was catapulted into the hallowed halls of fame. And then of course it was hard to know for sure if the person he met was into him, or merely attracted by the prospect of sharing his wealth and the attention that came with the job. And so he had quickly resorted to dating fellow actors, only to discover that jealousy and envy were all too real, and many couldn't cope with the fact that he was by far the most famous and most successful partner in the relationship.

And so after suffering through plenty of drama, he'd finally opted to stay single for a while, and effectively put that part of his life on hold. He missed being in a relationship, though. He missed the companionship, and the chance to share his life with someone. Which was part of the reason he was looking to make a big change, and maybe retreat from the limelight to some extent. Lead a normal life again. And maybe meet the woman of his dreams. It might still happen. He had to believe that it would. That it could.

He looked up when the same indie producer he met the night before joined him at the bar. "Had time to think about my proposal?" Howard asked straightaway.

"I have given it a lot of thought," he confirmed. "I even talked to my agent."

"And?" asked Howard, who looked fidgety, Tim thought. His pupils were also dilated, and he appeared to have taken some substance that didn't agree with him.

"He doesn't think it's a good idea. He's afraid it might be damaging to my career if I do an indie movie now." He shrugged. "I'm still interested, though."

"Good for you," said the producer, clapping him on the back. "Did you read the script I sent you?"

"I did. I like it. Especially the part of Craig Barnes."

"I knew it," said Howard, slamming the bar counter. "Did I tell you I wrote that part with you in mind?"

"You did?"

"Absolutely. Dream big, right? I just figured, if I wrote a part that you loved, and I got you attached to the project somehow, that would take care of my financing and I just might get the movie made. So how about it? Are you prepared to negotiate a deal?"

Tim laughed. "Hold your horses, buddy. We're not quite at that stage."

The guy frowned. "And why the hell not? You like the project. I'm telling you that with your name attached, financing is in the bag. So let's get this done."

"Not so fast. I can't do this without my agent's approval."

"To hell with your agent! What has he ever done for you?"

"Um, a lot, actually. He's the reason my career is where it is now."

"Look, I know you're raking in the millions right now," said the producer, tapping him in the chest with a bony finger. "But I'm talking integrity here, man. I'm talking artistic integrity—the kind that money can't buy. This movie is going to be seen by actual movie buffs—art lovers. Not just your usual popcorn-guzzling nitwits. If you do this movie, you'll get street cred. You'll get recognition from the people that matter. The people we got into the business of making movies for."

"I'm pretty sure that my audience loves movies, too," he said quietly. He didn't like all this talk about his fans being a bunch of popcorn-guzzling idiots. They might not be into the kind of artsy pictures the producer made, but if they were prepared to spend their hard-earned money to go see a movie, that meant something. It meant he'd made a movie that was worth spending your money on.

"Look, buddy boy," said Howard, poking his chest again, "you may be a star, and a big shot in the business, but in my world you have to earn the right to call yourself an actor. The fact that you're such a hotshot is actually working against you, see what I'm saying? My fans hate the kind of stuff you make. So you're going to have to work twice as hard to win them over. Not with that green screen crap that you're so fond of, but by showing some real acting chops—from the heart!"

He was pounding his chest now, and slurring his speech, and Tim had a hard time keeping the other man from touching his person. "I think you should take it easy, buddy," he said when the other man ordered another drink.

"Don't tell me to take it easy," the guy growled, swaying on his feet.

"It's just that this is a family place. And I don't think you should be drinking so much." Or taking whatever other substances he'd been indulging in.

"I'm fine," said Howard, waving an airy hand, then placing it on Tim's shoulder and putting his face very close to his. He could smell the liquor on the man's breath. "All I'm saying is that I can still give your part to some other actor. So don't think because you're the great Tim Deutch that this job is in the bag. It's not."

"I thought you said you wrote it for me?"

"I did. But now I'm thinking maybe I shouldn't have, you know. Seeing as how you're not as keen as I thought you would be."

"Oh, I'm keen," said Tim, though he had to admit he was having second thoughts now.

"Not keen enough!" said the producer. "You need to really want this, Timmy! You need to be willing to fight for this. If not, you're never going to be able to bring the passion this part wants—and you're going to lose out to some other, more deserving, more *hungry* actor."

"Oh, but I'm hungry," he said, and it was true. He'd been wanting to play a big, juicy part for so long now it was all he could think about. A part that meant something. That he could pour his heart and soul into. But he was suddenly starting to think that maybe this part wasn't it.

Howard must have sensed his reluctance, for he suddenly said, "You know what? Forget it. Forget I ever asked."

"But—"

"You don't deserve it, Timmy! You don't want it bad enough!"

And with these words, he grabbed his drink from the bar, sloshing part of the liquid on his shirt, and stumbled off, weaving his way through the crowd, too inebriated to walk straight.

Tim shook his head. So maybe this wasn't going to be as straightforward as he'd anticipated. He wanted to be a real actor again, but not if it involved having to work for the likes of Howard Jucha.

And so he turned back to face the bar, and felt oddly relieved.

Behind him on stage, the band had started playing, and that same singer from last night had taken the stage. He turned to watch. She was magnificent. What a voice. What a presence. And as her performance lit up the whole area, and her voice lifted his spirits and sent them soaring, he couldn't take his eyes off her. Who was this girl? And why had he never heard of her before?

CHAPTER 30

For the second night in a row, Olivia was fronting Due Course. The band's regular singer was a no-show again, and even though Shawn, the band's drummer, was reluctant to tell her about the reason for her absence, Olivia was grateful for the opportunity. She just loved to sing —always had, even when she was a little girl, when she was singing in her mother's choir back home. It was her whole life, and when she was singing, she could forget about the nastiness that had taken over her life of late—she could forget about everything—and simply be there.

And she was just getting warmed up when suddenly she spotted her mom and dad in the audience, and almost faltered. But she was professional enough not to let the sight of her parents phase her, and managed to carry on regardless.

They didn't look happy to see her, she thought. Especially her dad was looking at her as if he had some bone to pick with his daughter. And she could imagine what had happened. Pastor Dean must have gotten in touch with them, and told them about what happened, and asked them to talk to their daughter and tell her to fall in line or else. After all, if she was excommunicated, they would be under tremendous pressure to sever their connection with her… or also be expelled.

The song ended and she walked off stage, feeling a little dizzy from the combination of the high she often felt when performing in front of a crowd, and the anticipation of talking to her folks.

"Hey, you guys," she said, taking a seat at the table. "You should have told me you were coming."

"We wanted to surprise you," said her mom, leaning in to give her a kiss on the cheek. "What a wonderful performance, honey. I didn't know you had joined a band."

"I haven't. Not really," she said. "I'm just standing in for their regular singer. She couldn't be here tonight, so they asked me to give it a shot."

"You did great. But then of course you're always good with this kind of material." Mom's eyes were shiny, Olivia saw, and she wondered if she was happy to see her, or sad.

Her dad cleared his throat. "Some guy came to see us," he said. "Calls himself Diedrich. Said you got yourself into some kind of trouble with church leadership. They offered you some kind of deal but he says you said no." He fixed her with a hard look. "Can you tell us what this is all about? And why this guy came to us?"

"I felt he was threatening us," said Olivia's mom.

"He threatened you?" asked Olivia.

"It wasn't what he said, more the way he said it."

"He gave us the impression that you did something bad," her father grunted.

"I was wondering why you weren't singing with the choir anymore," said her mother. "You used to love to sing with them, and you were so good at it, too."

"This Diedrich fellow said you had decided to quit, and they want you back in a big way. He said that without you OceanPeak One just isn't the same, and I happen to agree. You are the heart of that choir. You're the only reason I listen to them in the first place."

She smiled. "Thanks, Dad," she said. That was such a sweet thing to say. Mostly because it just wasn't true. Her parents had always listened to OceanPeak One, long before she had joined them as their lead singer. In fact it was because of her parents that she became interested in the band. "They're not a choir, though," she said gently. It was a point of contention between her and her parents. They insisted a church choir shouldn't call itself a band. Even though OceanPeak One obviously was a band, not a choir.

"Whatever you want to call it, why did you quit?" asked her dad, still in that same gruff way of his.

She took a deep breath. She'd been avoiding this conversation, knowing that at some point she would have to face the music, so to speak. And now seemed as good a time as any. It was a conversation she clearly couldn't put off any longer.

"I didn't quit," she said. "I was fired. And also, excommunicated from the church."

Her parents exchanged worried glances. "What did you do?" asked her dad.

"I didn't do anything," she said. "I was attacked. Assaulted, actually. By Pastor Frank. And when I tried to say something about it, church leadership asked me to stay quiet, and suggested Pastor Frank and I talk about it, in the presence of a church mediator, and pray together. They stressed the importance of forgiveness, and didn't fail to point out that Pastor Frank is married and has a family and that my complaint could wreck his marriage and his career in the church. And so when I refused to keep quiet and allow Pastor

Frank to get away with what he did, they fired me from OceanPeak One and kicked me out of the church."

"God," said her mom, bringing a distraught hand to her face. "Honey, but why didn't you tell us about this?"

"I didn't want to upset you, Mom," she said.

"I knew something was wrong," said her mother. "Didn't I tell you something was wrong, Bill?"

"You did," said her dad, studying his daughter carefully. "So you're telling us that Pastor Frank assaulted you?"

"He did. One night after church, he was drunk and tried to kiss me and grope me. He cornered me and it was only when I kneed him in the groin that I managed to get away from him. I talked to others since, and turns out that wasn't the first time he did something like this. He has a reputation for being handsy, and for harassing young women." She was staring at her hands. "Most of these women kept quiet about it, for obvious reasons. Pastor Frank has Dean's backing, and who would believe a person telling these kinds of stories about him?"

"I hadn't heard these stories," said her mom uncertainly, as she sought her husband's gaze.

"I had," said Dad curtly. He was still looking angry, though Olivia was starting to think that maybe he wasn't angry with her after all. "There was a woman in our prayer group last year, who was telling a similar story that had played out with her daughter. The girl had left the church after that. Practically no one believed her, but her mother obviously did. She'd even filed an official complaint against Frank, but she said she hadn't heard back yet. She was still hoping they'd punish Frank for what he did to her daughter. Or at least demote him or something."

"So what happened? Did they demote him?" asked Olivia's mom.

"Obviously they didn't," Olivia murmured.

"Oh, no, that's right. He's still a pastor, isn't he?"

"He hasn't been punished for what he did," said her dad. "Though he should. Especially after what he did to you, honey." He reached out a hand and took hers. "You should have told us what happened. I would have gone and punched the guy's lights out if I'd known."

"I don't want you to go and punch Pastor Frank, Dad," said Olivia, touched by this unexpected display of support from one whose disappointment she'd feared.

"I want you to know that we stand by you one hundred percent," said her dad, squeezing her hand. "And if that means we're quitting the church, then so be it."

"Are we quitting the church?" asked her mom.

"We are," said her dad decidedly.

"But… why?"

"Because they kicked out our daughter when she wouldn't shut up about Frank being a jerk," her dad explained. "And if she doesn't keep her mouth shut, they're going to tell us we can't talk to her anymore either. She's excommunicated, and that means she won't exist anymore for church members in good standing."

"Oh, dear," said her mom, who had a hard time taking this all in.

"So either we quit this church," her dad continued, "or we lose our daughter. What's it going to be?"

"I don't want to lose Olivia," said her mom immediately. She thought for a moment, then her face cleared. "But what if they excommunicate Pastor Frank instead? Then we can all stay in the church, can't we?"

"They're not going to excommunicate Frank," said Dad. "That's why they sent this thug Diedrich to put the fear of God into us. Don't you see? They're circling the wagons—

that's what they're doing. They're not going to let what happened to Olivia stand in the way of Frank continuing to make a big career in the church."

"But... he's going to keep harassing women, won't he?"

"That doesn't seem to matter to them one bit," Olivia's dad growled. "Which is why we're quitting. And we're telling anyone who will listen exactly why we're quitting. We're not going to stay quiet about this. We're going to get really loud."

"But we'll lose all of our friends," said Mom, with a quiver in her voice.

"If these people won't talk to us anymore after what we have to say, that means they were never our friends to begin with," said Dad. He rubbed Olivia's back. "I just wish you would have told us sooner, honey."

Olivia wiped away a tear. "I was afraid you'd be upset."

"Of course we're upset. And we have every right to be upset. This man is an animal, sweetie, and he has to be stopped, before more people get hurt."

"And to think I always liked Pastor Frank," Mom mused. "He's so handsome."

"My God, woman," Dad muttered, and shook his head in amazement.

"Well, he is. He's got the most handsome face... but a dark heart," she added, and held out her arms to hug her daughter. "Oh, honey. It's so brave, what you did."

Olivia hugged her mom, and when her dad joined in, she felt the tears stream down her face. She hadn't expected this. She hadn't expected her parents to support her like this, and take her side in this conflict. But their support meant so much to her—it meant the world.

"Did you really kick him in the groin?" asked Mom finally, when they had broken the group hug and she and Olivia were drying their eyes with paper napkins.

"I did," she confirmed. "A nice big kick in the family jewels."

"Oh, dear."

Dad winked at her. "That's my girl."

CHAPTER 31

It was getting late, and Olivia's mom and dad decided to retire for the night. But Olivia was feeling so uplifted that she didn't think she would be able to get to sleep, so she wanted to stick around for a little while longer. Maybe take a long walk along the beach.

Before her mom left, she gave her a hug and said, "When you were a little girl, you loved singing so much that I knew this was going to be a big part of your life. And I was right, wasn't I? When you were singing in your choir—or your band—your dad and I were always so very proud. He would never say it, but I could see it in his eyes."

There was a pang of sorrow as she thought she would never be singing for OceanPeak One ever again. "I'm sorry about what happened, Mom," she said.

"Don't be," said her mom, then suddenly turned fierce. "You have nothing to be sorry about. On the contrary."

"But I'll never be able to sing again," she said. "I'll never be able to make you proud."

"Don't be silly. Nobody owns your voice, honey. There will be other opportunities for you to sing. Better opportunities. And for people who truly appreciate you, and don't want to silence you, like these people tried to do." She gave her arm a squeeze. "We could never be more proud of you than we are right now. Remember that."

And with these words, they went to bed, promising to share breakfast together the next morning, and talk about what Olivia's future might hold.

She settled in, and wondered if Due Course would need her services again tomorrow night. And as she checked her messages, a young man approached her table. He stood politely gazing down at her, and just as she was thinking that he looked familiar somehow, he asked, "Could I join you for just a moment, miss?"

She was too much taken aback to say no, figuring he was probably a fan wanting a selfie or an autograph, but when he took the seat her mom had vacated, he said, "I couldn't help but overhear part of your conversation earlier. I'm sorry—I promise you I wasn't eavesdropping. I was sitting at the next table, and some of the things you said made a deep impression on me. As did your performance earlier tonight."

She wasn't too well pleased that some stranger had been listening in on her private conversation with her parents, but then again, this was a public space, and they had probably been talking too loudly, so she couldn't really blame him.

"I'm sorry," he said, registering her dismay. "You're upset. So I won't keep you too long. I just wanted to say that you did the right thing by breaking away from that church. If they want to muzzle you, and threatened your parents, they deserve to be held accountable." He got up again. "Oh, and also, your voice—it really touched me. You're an amazing talent, Olivia. Just so you know." He flashed her a smile. "And now I'll leave you in peace. Have a nice evening."

And then it hit her. "You're Tim Deutch, aren't you?"

He hesitated. "Guilty as charged," he conceded. "I hope you won't hold it against me."

She laughed. "God, I love your movies, Mr. Deutch. And so does my dad."

He quirked an eyebrow. "And your mom?"

"Not so much," she admitted.

"Thought so. Something I have to work on."

"Please, don't leave," she said.

"I really shouldn't have listened in on your conversation."

"No, it's fine. I shouldn't have discussed a private matter in such a public place." He lowered himself into the chair again, and she added, "I didn't recognize you at first. How do you do that? How do you disguise yourself without actually using a disguise?"

"I'm glad you ask. I have absolutely no idea. But I'm glad it's working."

It wasn't really working—she just hadn't been paying attention to other people, too absorbed in her own problems. But as he pulled a ball cap deep over his eyes, and sank lower into his chair, she watched him simply disappear.

"How about now?" he asked.

"Perfect. Completely invisible."

"Good. I love my fans, but taking selfies all the time gets really exhausting after a while, especially when you're trying to enjoy a nice meal, or strike up a conversation with an amazingly talented young lady like yourself."

He was charming, there was no doubt about that. And he was very easy to talk to, and so before she realized, she was relating the whole story of Pastor Frank to him in great detail, and when she was done, he told her about life in the fast lane, and how he'd come to Hampton Cove to get away from the pressure and the stress for a while. And now that he said it, she did notice the rings under his eyes.

"You look tired," she said.

"That's because I am tired. Dead tired."

"Wanna go for a walk?" she suggested.

"I thought you'd never ask."

They spent the next hour walking along the beach, and talking nonstop. She couldn't remember ever having opened up to such an extent to anyone. She had met some great guys in the church, and had hung out with several of them over the years she'd been a member. But she'd never experienced this easy rapport. And so pretty soon she didn't see Tim as a movie star, but as just a regular guy, which he was, much to her surprise. By the time they were on their way back to the resort, it was almost as if they'd known each other all of their lives.

"I had a great time," she said as they stood in front of her room.

"Yeah, me too," he said. "Thanks for the walk—and the company—and the conversation. And please, whatever you do, never stop singing, Olivia. You're such an amazing talent. You can't let that go."

"I won't," she promised. "I understand now that my singing doesn't have anything to do with the church. And so leaving the church shouldn't stop me from doing what I've always loved best." It was just that in her mind, and because she'd been a member of the church for so long, singing was always associated with being part of that community. But now she saw that it was actually part of who she was. And being expelled or excommunicated shouldn't stop her from being who she was—and from singing. "And you shouldn't limit your experience to just doing these big movies," she said. "You can do both. You really can."

Tim nodded thoughtfully. "You're right. There are plenty of actors who pursue both directions in their careers. Who play big successful movies, and in between they also play parts in smaller, more serious-minded movies. One doesn't exclude the other." He took a curt bow. "Thanks for pointing that out to me, Miss Hill."

"You're welcome, Mr. Deutch."

They stood together for a moment, then Tim gave her a quick kiss on the cheek, and they said their goodbyes. For now.

It really had been a magical night, and somehow Olivia felt, as she stepped into her room, that the world had suddenly turned a little brighter. And filled with possibility.

CHAPTER 32

Cole Newman was ready to start another day. If he wondered if today would be his last working day at the resort, he didn't dwell on it. If the resort went belly-up, so be it. If not, he'd gladly keep working there for the rest of his professional life. He'd already given so much, and had received so much in return, he hoped to extend the experience for as long as he was given the chance.

He'd been thinking a lot about Grace, of course. Their brief reunion had stirred something in him that he'd thought dead and buried. That old flame was still burning. The embers must have been kept aflame for all these years, and Grace's renewed presence in his life had suddenly breathed new life into them.

He didn't know whether that was a good thing or not. He'd turned pining for Grace Wheeler into an art form many years ago, when she'd suddenly disappeared from his life without so much as a goodbye. Apparently he didn't matter much to her then, and he had no reason to think he would matter to her now. In fact she hadn't even recognized him at first, though his new, more hirsute appearance might have had something to do with that. At first he'd grown the beard figuring he looked too youthful and babyfaced to be appreciated by the ladies. Now he kept it out of sheer laziness. Plus, it made him look older—never a bad thing when you want to project professionalism and competence in your job.

Not that there was ever a question about his competence. If it wasn't for Cole, this resort would have stopped running a long time ago. In fact it was his skillfulness that kept the place going, and had saved them a lot of money in repairs over the years. Though he had to admit that some of these systems were in great need of replacement. He was a great handyman, but he wasn't a miracle worker, after all.

And as he walked past reception, on his way to his office, he suddenly wondered if Grace had remembered to follow up with Terry and Heather. He passed the breakfast room, and glanced in. Plenty of people, but no Terry or Heather. So he set foot for Grace's office, hoping the big boss would be in at such an early hour. Much to his surprise, she was. Johnny had mostly been a no-show in the final years of his tenure, though Michele had done an excellent job as his replacement.

"Did you get a chance to talk to the Davis couple?" he asked, bursting into Grace's office without knocking, as was his habit.

"Don't you ever knock?" asked Grace, looking annoyed.

"The Davises?" he repeated.

She frowned. "Remind me, who are they again?"

"Terry and Heather Davis. They're having financial difficulties?"

"Oh, right. No, I'm afraid I didn't have time to talk to them yesterday."

At least she hadn't kicked them out, as she had apparently been wanting to do the day before. He didn't want to say it, but his impression was that her years spent working in Silicon Valley had made Grace Wheeler hard of heart.

She returned to whatever she was doing, but he decided to wait her out this time. He had the impression that if he didn't push her, the Davises would be at the back of her mind the moment he left.

And so he stood there, until she finally looked up again.

"What?" she said, her voice dripping with annoyance.

"Let's go see them now," he suggested.

"Cole, please. I have more important things on my mind right now."

"You were never like this before, you know. At least not that I remember."

"Not like what?" she asked, returning to her computer screen and shifting her mouse this way and that.

"Indifferent. Cold. Not interested in other people."

She blinked and finally abandoned whatever she was working on. She gave him a vague smile. "Cold, indifferent and not interested in people. Wow, Cole. And you got all that from the five minutes we've spent together, did you?"

"It's true," he said. "You don't seem to care about the Davises."

"And I don't care about you, isn't that what you're saying?"

He shrugged. "That was a long time ago," he murmured.

"Not that long. Not long enough for me not to remember." She sat up a little straighter, supporting her head with her hands. "Tell me what's really on your mind, will you? Cause this isn't about the Davids couple, that much I can tell."

"Davis, not Davids."

"This is about me leaving, isn't it?"

"Look, can we just go and look in on them? I'm worried."

"This is about me leaving and not saying goodbye to you."

"Water under the bridge," he said, rubbing his bushy beard.

"We never were an item, Cole. We had a couple of dates, we kissed, and that's it. We were seventeen, for crying out loud!"

"Eighteen, but whatever."

"You act as if we were on the verge of getting married, and I suddenly broke up with you. We didn't break up, cause we were never actually together."

"Ouch," he said.

She frowned. "And besides, it was your decision not to go to college. We could have been together, but you preferred to stay here and work for my dad."

"I didn't go to college because my parents couldn't afford it. And besides, I love my job. I love working here. Your dad was a wonderful boss—until he couldn't be bothered anymore and gave up." He sighed. "Look, can we just go and talk to Terry and Heather, check to see if they're fine? I'm really worried about them, all right?"

"Okay, fine. Let's go," she said, and swiftly got to her feet. And as they passed out of her office, she scrutinized him for a brief moment, before saying, "I'm not sure about the beard, though, Cole."

"I don't care. It's my beard. And it doesn't say anywhere in my contract that I can't have one."

"Some men look good with a beard. You, I'm afraid to say, do not, my friend."

"Lay off the beard," he said, though he had to smile at the back-and-forth. It reminded him of old times. But then he sobered. What old times? According to her, they hadn't even been an item. So apparently there were no old times.

They arrived at the room occupied by the old couple, and Grace held up her hand to knock, but then paused. "What do I tell them? I can't just barge in there and start jabbering about their finances. That's just plain rude. Not to mention an invasion of their privacy. It might even be illegal."

"Tell them they won a prize."

"What prize?"

"Tell them they won a prize and you're going to comp their room."

"You're crazy. If we're going to allow everyone to stay here for free, this resort will go down the tubes faster than you can say 'comp.' And besides, you need to enter a competition before you can win a prize. They may be old, but they're not senile. They'll know something is going on."

Cole thought for a moment. "Tell them the resort is celebrating its fiftieth anniversary, and since they're honored guests who've been coming here since the beginning, you're going to comp the room."

"Stop saying 'comp,' Cole!"

"We have to do something, Grace!"

"Oh, for God's sakes," Grace muttered, and knocked on the door.

"What are you going to tell them?"

"I don't know. I'll think of something."

"Great strategy."

She knocked again, but there was no answer.

"I think they're out," she said.

"They're not in the breakfast room."

"So? Maybe they had an early breakfast and they're on the beach already."

"I doubt it. They keep to a strict schedule. They should be having breakfast right now."

"And you know this, how, exactly?"

"I know this because I take an interest in people," he said. "And also, I've been here for so long now I know the daily routines of all the regulars by heart." He would also have mentioned that he preferred to fix whatever was broken when people were out, and so he knew where they would be and when, but Grace had knocked again, and this time he thought he heard a noise from inside the room.

"Did you hear that?" she asked, pressing her ear to the door.

"They're in there, all right," said Cole, and suddenly started to fear the worst. People like the Davises, finding themselves in dire straits, just might resort to taking drastic measures. Like taking their own lives.

And so he took out his master key.

"You can't go in there," said Grace.

"Watch me," he said, and opened the door.

It took some time to register what they saw. Terry and Heather Davis were lying on the bed, their eyes closed, and holding hands. They were very pale, and instinctively Cole knew they weren't asleep. Then his eyes traveled to a pill bottle on the nightstand. An empty pill bottle.

"Call an ambulance," he said immediately, as he hurried over to the bed, and felt for a pulse. "Call an ambulance!" he repeated when Grace just stood there, watching the couple with dread written all over her face.

He felt a pulse, very weak, on Terry, and the same on Heather. And so he started doing CPR, first on Terry, then on the man's wife.

"How could they do this!" said Grace.

"Did you call?"

She nodded, looking distinctly distressed.

"Can you work on Heather while I work on Terry?"

She nodded again, and at his instigation, and following his instructions, she mimicked the procedure he was applying to Terry. It might just keep them both alive long enough for the paramedics to arrive.

CHAPTER 33

Grace was pacing up and down the hospital corridor. Terry and Heather Davis had been taken there by ambulance, with Grace and Cole traveling behind them in Cole's car. Cole had shoved aside a pile of junk and old bills and candy bar wrappers to make space for Grace, and they'd traveled the short journey in silence, both too deeply impressed by what had just happened to talk.

And now they were waiting for news about the couple.

"I don't understand why they would do this," said Grace, as she gratefully accepted a cup of hot coffee from Cole.

"Their financial problems must have been worse than we thought," said Cole as he took a seat on the plastic chair.

Grace couldn't sit. She couldn't remain still, like Cole. "I don't get it. If you can't pay your bills, talk to someone. Don't just swallow a bottle of pills and drift off."

"I can tell you probably never had financial problems in your life," said Cole.

Grace turned on him. "Are you kidding me right now? When did this become about me, all of a sudden?"

"It's not," he said. "I apologize. But you could have talked to them sooner. Like yesterday, when I told you to."

"If you haven't noticed, I'm under a great deal of pressure right now. My dad sold the resort right from under us, and now my ex-boss, the one who fired me and destroyed my career, turns out to be the new owner, and he's got all these great plans for the resort that will probably wreck the place and turn it into the Argent—only worse. Some... synthetic, ugly, heartless, soulless..."

"Your dad sold the resort?"

"He did, yeah. And he didn't even bother to tell us. Or Mom. Who's technically the owner, but that didn't stop him." She plunked herself down on a chair. "Dad had lost interest in the resort, and had been spending a lot of money, rewarding himself for what he felt was a missed career as an engineer, which he blamed on Mom's family. So he took what he felt he was owed, and spent the money on expensive cars, yachts, vacations, and a mistress—Mom's best friend Juda."

Cole had heard some of this from Hazel, but he didn't know all the details. He wasn't into gossip the way some of the staff were, and usually kept himself to himself and tried to stay out of all of that stuff. But if what Grace was saying was true, this was bad. "So this guy Solys, or Polys, or whatever his name is, he wants to turn us into the Argent?"

"He does. And then he wants to create a bunch of clones and put them all over the world."

"He wants to franchise the concept."

Grace nodded. "Mom told me to play nice, or else Polys might pull out, and then we're sunk." She threw up her hands. "Dad broke us, Cole. He destroyed us."

"But why? Just because he felt frustrated?"

She nodded. "We can't ask him, because he's gone, but that's what it looks like."

"I knew he lost interest when he stopped showing up, and left the running of the resort to Michele—who did an amazing job, by the way."

"I know. But it would have been nice if she'd told us about some of this. Then maybe we could have intervened before it was too late."

"Your dad was a great boss," said Cole, stretching out his legs. "He was more a friend than a boss, and so in some people's books he was probably a bad boss. He was very kind, you know. Always had your back. I liked him a lot, actually."

Grace smiled. "Dad was an engineer. He loved solving problems. He had no interest in being anybody's boss or being in charge."

"I know. We could spend hours in his office discussing solutions to some problem with the pool, or the resort's water supply. He loved that kind of stuff. But then over time he seemed to grow tired of the whole thing."

"Why was that, you think?"

"My best guess is that he hated running the show. Like you said, your dad loved solving complicated technical problems, and coming up with ingenious solutions. What he didn't like was dealing with staffing issues, the mountain of admin that comes with the territory, tax stuff, permissions, politics, and the kind of people management you need to be good at when you're dealing with guests."

"Dad did not like the guests," said Grace with a smile. "He used to say the resort would be the perfect place to work at, if only he could get rid of the guests."

"I know. He kept avoiding them. Whenever a guest asked for the manager, your dad was nowhere to be found. I think he escaped through the back entrance. He hated confrontation, and he hated having to deal with angry people, or any of the great number of issues you run into when you're in the hospitality business."

"He was a great dad, but a lousy manager," said Grace with a sigh. "He probably thought he was doing the right thing when he sold the resort to Polys. He must have known he was my boss, and probably figured he was our best bet to ensure the resort's future. He trusted him." Little did he know that Polys wasn't the guy everyone thought he was. The man was probably evil personified.

"Is it true that your dad was having an affair with Juda Andrews?"

"They were together when he died. My mom walked in on them, and the shock must have been so great his heart gave out on him. Juda now claims Dad had promised her he'd divorce Mom and marry her."

"Your dad's life had become pretty messy."

"And he was hiding it so well. From Mom, but also from us. Every time we came over for the holidays, he would act as if nothing was wrong. But this must have been eating at him. Until he ran out of time and his heart stopped. He could have said something, you know. About how unhappy he was. About the way he felt that life had pulled a nasty trick on him, and how he was trying to make up for it. Almost as if he was trying to create a new life—while still holding on to the old one."

"Leading a double life. That must have been pretty stressful for him."

A doctor approached, and they both got up.

"How are they?" asked Grace immediately.

"Good news. We got there just in time," said the doctor. "We pumped their stomachs, and they won't have any lasting damage from the pills they took. They're resting now, but they'll be fine."

"Can we see them?" asked Grace.

The doctor hesitated, but then nodded. "Make it brief."

They entered the room, and saw that Terry and Heather

were side by side in separate hospital beds. They had their eyes closed, but the moment Grace and Cole walked in, they looked up. They both looked embarrassed, Grace thought.

"My name is Grace Wheeler," Grace began.

"We know who you are, sweetie," said Heather.

"We've known you from when you were born," Terry added.

Grace smiled and took a seat next to the nearest bed, which was Heather's. "You should have told me what was going on," she said. "I would have tried to help."

"We didn't think anyone could help us," said Heather sadly.

"We don't want to be a burden to anyone," Terry explained.

"How could you ever be a burden?" said Grace, greatly touched by the experience. "Cole overheard you talking about some financial trouble you're in?"

"Eavesdropping, huh, Cole?" said Terry.

"I just happened to catch your conversation," Cole muttered.

"We lost all of our savings, and the house, to a crook," said Heather.

"Our banker told us to diversify our investment portfolio," said Terry. "Said the real estate market was hot right now, and we would get a great price for the house, which was getting too big for us anyway, and too expensive in upkeep. If we sold the house now and invested the money, we could pay the rent on a nice little apartment for the rest of our lives. And so he gave us a card from some investment adviser, who told us to invest everything in something called bitcoin. He said we would easily triple our investment, and then we'd be set for life."

"Whatever was left of our lives, anyway," said Heather, who coughed.

"And so we foolishly trusted this guy, and gave him permission to invest our savings, and the money we got from the sale of the house. For a while he kept sending us monthly reports, telling us everything was going well. The bitcoin was up, and we were doing great. But then suddenly the reports stopped coming."

"When we didn't hear from him, and we couldn't reach him on the phone, we asked our banker. Turns out he'd been arrested for fraud, and his accounts were all being investigated. And the bitcoin guy had also been arrested."

"There were no investments. There was no bitcoin. It was one big hole," said Terry. "And all of our money was gone, along with the money of dozens of others."

"So now we don't have anything left," said Heather. "No house, no money, and we can't even afford to pay rent anymore."

"Don't you have your pensions?" asked Grace.

"We do, but it's not enough to pay for everything."

"Which is why we figured we might as well end things," said Terry.

"We don't have kids—no family to speak of," said Heather.

"We have each other, and that's always been enough," said Terry, and reached out a hand across the gap between the beds. Heather took it and they shared a look of such love and fondness it brought tears to Grace's eyes.

She swallowed away a lump in her throat. "What did you do before you retired?"

"I was a gardener," said Terry.

"Not just a gardener," said Heather. "Terry owned his own company. He had six people working under him."

"You had more people working for you. Heather ran the housekeeping department at the Hartford, a small hotel in Queens, where we live. Or at least where we used to live," he added on a somber note.

Grace shared a look with Cole, who was rubbing his beard again, a habit he seemed to have picked up along with growing the darn thing. "You know, the Hampton Cove is going through some major changes right now," she said. "I don't know if you've heard, but my dad died, and a new investor is coming in, and my sisters and I have taken on some of the responsibilities of running the resort."

"I'm sorry to hear about your dad," said Heather sincerely.

"He was a great guy," said Terry. "Really loved that place."

"So we're looking for a couple of very specific profiles right now," said Grace.

"What profiles? What are you talking about?" asked Terry.

"Well, I just heard we lost our gardener, who quit. And we also lost the person in charge of housekeeping. Both of them have been hired by the Argent." Just like Michele and probably many others. "Which means we're looking for a gardener, and also someone to run the housekeeping department." She held up a hand when both Terry and Heather started to speak. "Just for the time being," she said. "I understand you're both retired, and you may not want to go back to work at your age. But if you would, you'd be doing us a huge favor. It's hard to find great people on short notice. The labor market is really tight right now, and we're not exactly the most prestigious place to work at, and that's obviously a major consideration for many people. These would be paying positions, of course," she added, just in case there was any doubt about that.

She found two pairs of eyes staring up at her in great surprise.

"We're not *that* old," said Terry finally.

"You would do that for us?" asked Heather, greatly touched.

"It's not a favor," Grace explained. "It's a job."

Heather eyed her husband, who said, "There's still life in

these bones of mine, and I only sold my business because I thought I'd fetch a good price, which I did."

"I don't mind returning to my old job, as long as I don't have to get down on my hands and knees to clean up the vomit of some young hoodlums," said Heather.

"We don't get hoodlums at the Hampton Cove," said Cole. "Only nice and decent people like you."

This had Terry and Heather smiling. And the latter had tears in her eyes when she said, "I'll take the job, Miss Wheeler."

"Grace, please."

"I'll also take the job," Terry confirmed. "Which probably means we should call you boss from now on?"

Grace wasn't so sure about that. Could be that Polys would be the boss, and she would be sidelined. Again. But she nodded. "But you can still call me Grace."

"Just like your dad," said Heather with a smile. "He always said we should call him Johnny."

"He said we were his favorite guests," said Terry. "Because we didn't complain, and we didn't make a mess of our room."

"Well, that's settled then," said Grace. "You're both hired as of now. Welcome to the team."

Two faces beamed up at her. "Thank you, Grace," said Heather.

"You're welcome," she said, and then excused herself, for she was tearing up again herself. Tough to be a boss if you are going to burst into tears all the time.

CHAPTER 34

They'd left the hospital, where Heather and Terry would have to stay overnight to keep them under observation. Cole had promised to come pick them up tomorrow, and Grace said they could rest and recover as long as they needed to.

But both seemed eager to get to work, and Grace had the impression she would have to stop them or they would report for duty the next morning.

"Did our gardener really quit?" asked Cole.

"He did, actually. And so did the head of housekeeping."

"That was very kind of you," said Cole.

"Are you saying now that I might have a heart, after all?"

"I never said you didn't. I just said you might have lost it."

He had a point, though. Working for Polys, she might have lost some of that humanity and some of those values her parents had instilled in her. Silicon Valley was a cutthroat place, and a tough working environment, and being VP to a man like Jay Polys probably hadn't done her a lot of good. Which reminded her of something. "It's entirely possible Polys will take over as general manager. And if that happens, things at the Hampton Cove are going to change, Cole. And not, I'm afraid, for the better. He's a tough boss, and he's going to change the way we do things around here. Terry and Heather might not be able to stick around very long."

"I might not stick around if Polys takes over," said Cole. "Though I would like to. I've worked here my entire adult life, and the place has become home to me, and my colleagues and some of the guests almost like family."

"I know," said Grace, eyeing the handyman with concern. If they lost Cole, and Hazel, and Steven, and Nicolas, soon no one would be left. The resort was emptying out, and with these trusty workers, the place would also lose its soul.

"So what are your plans?" asked Cole as they leaned against his car, which was a decrepit old thing, but still ran pretty well. "Are you going to stay on? Or leave for San Francisco the first chance you get?"

"I'm afraid that you'll be stuck with me for a while," said Grace. And she related to him the events that had led to her dismissal. Cole seemed pretty shocked when she told him the whole story. He even got worked up when she mentioned the ethics report. Which endeared him to her, she had to admit. "So you see, I'm unhirable right now, and my best guess is that this will stay that way. And by the time people have forgotten about what happened, a new generation will have taken over, and I'll be too old for Silicon Valley."

"You could find a job elsewhere. It's a big country."

"I don't know, Cole. I was thinking that maybe it's time to come home, you know. I don't even remember why I left, but whatever the reason was, it's gone now." And the same thing seemed to apply to her sisters. Though she wouldn't bet on Jill hanging around once she got some bee in her bonnet about some new spiritual place-to-be she needed to check out, or some guru who could lead her to enlightenment.

Lauren, though, was probably not moving back to New York. Unless of course Jack's music career crashed and burned.

"So if I stick around, and you stick around, does that mean we're stuck with each other?" asked Cole, and when she looked up sharply, she saw that his eyes were smiling, and his beard was twitching.

"I guess so," she said.

"Your leaving, that didn't have anything to do with me, did it?"

"It didn't. As far as I can remember, it had more to do with Mom. She's mellowed out a lot over the years, but she used to be pretty difficult to put up with back in the day. And to live with." Mom had been controlling, and very strict about the way they looked, the way they behaved, and always concerned with the way people thought about their family. Now, though, with everything that had happened, she couldn't care less, which was actually a nice change of pace.

"Your mom was pretty strict," Cole agreed. "She didn't like me, for one thing. Didn't think I was the right person for you."

"She said that?"

"She didn't have to. It was pretty clear from the way she looked at me."

"You were probably not rich enough," said Grace. "Mom always looked up to people richer than us, and down on people who were poorer. Luckily that doesn't seem to be the case anymore. She's lost some of her snobbishness."

This whole business with Juda and Dad had been a great shock to Mom. And perhaps it had opened her eyes to the things that really matter in life: not how much money you have in your bank account, or the kind of clothes you wear, or the house you live in, but the kind of person you are. Though apparently Mom had reconciled with Juda, which was a good thing, for Juda was good people.

Cole cleared his throat. "So if you're going to be around for a while, could I..."

"Could you what?"

"Could I maybe ask you out sometime? If you're not seeing anyone right now, I mean."

"I'm not seeing anyone right now," Grace confirmed, touched by this fumbling way of asking her out. She studied her old boyfriend for a moment. She'd lied, of course, when she said they'd never dated. They had, and for a while she'd thought Cole was her future. But then she'd had the opportunity to go to college, which would take her away from her parents—her mother mainly—and she desperately wanted to say yes. Only Cole hadn't wanted to join her. He'd already started working for her dad, and loved it. And so she had to make a decision.

She knew they wouldn't make it if she left, even though Cole seemed to think they could make it work. But she had no intention of coming back as often as he hoped. And if he wouldn't join her, there really was no future for them.

And so finally she'd gone for her dream, and he had stayed behind. They'd still seen each other whenever she came home for the holidays, but less and less. And anyway, she'd started a different life the moment she started college: new friends, new opportunities, new prospects. And Cole became part of her past. A past she didn't enjoy being reminded of, because mixed in with the good, there were the things she'd escaped from, and so she'd gradually erased him from her mind, and her heart.

But here he was, alive and well, and willing to take another chance on them.

"I would go out on a date with you, Cole," she said finally. "But I can't."

He looked disappointed. "So you *are* seeing someone."

"No, I'm not." She eyed him amusedly. "It's the beard."

"The beard?"

"If you were willing to give up the beard, I might be inclined to say yes."

"You want me to shave off the beard?" he asked, touching the hideous thing.

"I do, yes. I hate beards, Cole. Especially your beard, which looks like the kind of thing you might find in the shower drain."

He looked hurt, but only for a moment. "Done," he said.

"No more beard?"

"Consider it gone."

"I'm still reserving judgment, though."

"You're hedging your bets?"

"Hey, I'm figuring there must be a reason you grew that thing."

"You're thinking I've got something horrible hiding underneath the beard?"

"I do, yes. And it might jump out at me the moment you shave off the beard."

He laughed, a wonderful sound. "Okay, so I'll shave, and present myself to you for inspection. Then, and only then will you be expected to say yes or no. How is that?"

"That sounds like a great idea."

They got into the car. "You could have ordered me to shave the beard," he said. "You are my boss now, after all."

"Okay, fine. Cole Newman, I'm ordering you to shave—for hygienic purposes, obviously. And also esthetic ones. Can't have the resort maintenance man scaring the guests by popping up looking like Bigfoot."

"I don't look like Bigfoot."

"You do, actually."

"You haven't changed a thing, Grace."

Which was actually funny, for he'd said the opposite thing just that morning. So she settled back in her seat, surrounded by her old boyfriend's detritus of years spent as a bachelor, and found herself relaxing for the first time in a while.

He started up the car, and a tune started blasting from the speaker. It sounded a lot like the kind of music he'd been listening to when they were still dating.

"Sorry about that," he murmured, and turned down the volume.

And as she studied him while he expertly navigated the hospital parking lot and started on their return home, she thought he actually looked pretty butch with the beard. Pretty irresistible. But of course she would never tell him that.

CHAPTER 35

In strong contrast with the previous days, the next week at the Hampton Cove Resort & Spa passed uneventfully as Grace took up her position at the helm of the family business, supported by her sisters and the rest of her staff. There were no more staff members quitting their job, and the positions that were open were quickly filled. A big surprise came the second week, when Bea Wheeler decided to step back into the business and become the resort's PR person. It was a welcome addition to the team, as Bea had some great ideas to put the resort on the map again, and attract new guests. She had an innovative approach that was still in line with the way the resort had sold itself over the years as a place for families.

Contrary to Grace's fear that her sister would abandon them for the next shiny toy in the land of spiritual enlightenment, Jill had thrown herself into her new role as the resort's fitness instructor and yoga teacher with gusto. She loved her new job and she was good at it, branching out into daily aqua gym classes for the elderly, and variations of tai chi and qigong for the same age group. Her classes were always packed to capacity, and the enthusiasm and energy she brought to them proved infectious, as her attendance levels clearly showed.

Lauren was proving to be an effective and popular customer relations officer, giving the guests a person to talk to about possible grievances, and enjoying her new position. All in all it was clear that with this renewed presence of the Wheeler family at the helm, the resort had received a much-needed boost, and their dedication to returning to the days when the resort had been a jewel amongst the state's beach resorts was felt by all—staff and guests alike.

Jay Polys, meanwhile, even though on paper the majority shareholder now, and so effectively the owner, had decided to adopt a hands-off approach. His frequent run-ins with Grace had made him weary of playing the more active role he'd envisioned for himself, and he was happy to take a wait-and-see approach. He kept his ear to the ground, and visited frequently, even while trying to be discreet about it, and often sending in a proxy to determine how the Wheelers were doing. Nicolas Holmes, the resort accountant, reported both to him and Grace, and so Polys had a good overview of the financial situation at the resort, its occupancy rate, which he followed up daily, and customer satisfaction ratings, information he gleaned from Lauren, who kept him up to date via email on that all-important data.

And so it was that two weeks into the Wheeler sisters' tenure, Steven was chatting with Hazel when he saw two familiar faces passing through his lobby. They were Tim Deutch and Olivia Hill, and they were walking arm in arm, bright smiles on their faces.

"Will you look at that," said Steven wistfully. "Young love. Doesn't it just make you sick?"

Hazel, who had joined him at the reception desk for a chat, prior to returning to her office, gave her young colleague a curious look. "Someone got up on the wrong side of the bed this morning."

"No, but it's true, isn't it? Some people have all the luck. Take Tim Deutch, for instance. Not only did Variety post that he's the best-paid actor of his generation, but he's also clearly in love with this Olivia Hill person, whoever she is."

"Olivia Hill is a very accomplished singer, and if you spent your evenings at the resort instead of going clubbing, you would know that."

Steven made a face. "I spend all day at this place. Why would I want to spend my nights here, too?"

"Because it's a great place, with a great ambiance? And the band Olivia is fronting is probably one of the hottest bands on the East Coast right now. In fact it wouldn't surprise me if they weren't snapped up for some big record deal soon."

"Who cares?" Steven grumbled.

Hazel gave him a solicitous pat on the arm. "No more messages from your secret admirer, I take it?"

"Nothing. After bombarding me with messages for days, it's been a whole week now without even a single one. It's almost as if he—or she—I'm still not discounting the possibility that this is a female who's been hounding me, mistakenly believing I would ever consider romance with a member of her species—has ceased to exist." He sighed deeply. "Or else he simply lost interest. I think that's probably the most likely scenario. Oh well, it was nice while it lasted. Though I would very much like to have known who this person was. Simply to satisfy my own personal curiosity."

Just at that moment, Nicolas traipsed through the reception area, caught sight of Hazel and Steven, and quickly returned to his office. He had all the hallmarks of a trepidatious mouse, scared of its own shadow.

"Hold on to that thought," said Hazel, and went in pursuit of the timid accountant.

"Hold on to what?" asked Steven, surprised by the speed with which his colleague was removing herself from the scene. "Where are you going?"

Hazel caught up with Nicolas just as he was entering his office, and he was about to close the door in her face when she put her foot in the opening and forced her way in. "What do you think you're playing at?" she hissed, none too friendly.

"What are you talking about?" he asked, not meeting her gaze.

"First you keep bombarding that poor kid with love notes, and then all of a sudden the big nothing? Why are you ghosting Steven?"

"I'm not ghosting Steven. I just didn't see the point of this anymore, that's all." He glanced up at her, then down again when he met her fiery gaze. "He doesn't want me, so why continue the charade?"

"What are you talking about?"

"I overheard him talking to Jill last week. They were talking about boyfriends, and she told him she's into the athletic type and Steven confirmed that he's into athletic men also." He lightly patted his belly, which was on the rotund side. "Do I look athletic to you? I'm a butterball, Hazel. I'm the opposite of athletic. So I decided not to fool myself into thinking Steven might be into me, and just drop the whole thing. Spare myself the heartache. And possibly creating an awkward atmosphere when he found out it was me who was sending him those poems."

"First off, you're not a butterball," said Hazel, who saw she needed to do some straight talking to her colleague. "Are you ready to compete in the Olympics? No. But then none of us are. Steven isn't a star athlete either. And I think you two would be perfectly compatible. And second, how can you tell he's not into you if you haven't even told him you like him? You're not even giving him a chance!"

"I know what I saw," said Nicolas stubbornly. "He likes me as a friend. As a colleague. He'll never see me as anything more than that."

"How do you know that, if you don't tell him how you feel!"

"I don't have to tell him. I can see it in his eyes when he talks to me. Casual, you know. But without the simmering passion lurking at the heart of his being."

"God," said Hazel, putting a distraught hand to her brow. "You're even more of a diva than he is."

"Steven is not a diva," said Nicolas decidedly. "Steven is... simply wonderful."

"Of course he is. But so are you." She came to a swift decision. "Look, if you're not going to tell him, I will."

The accountant's eyes went wide in horror and shock. "But you promised!"

"I know I did, but that was before you proved a great disappointment."

"I know I'm a disappointment," said the accountant, now slumping in his chair. "Which is probably why Steven doesn't like me. Nobody likes me."

"Oh, for crying out loud," said Hazel, who'd had enough of this. "Stop whining, or I'll kick your butt so hard you won't be able to sit straight for a week. Now are you going to tell Steven or am I going to have to do it for you?"

"Please don't tell him. I'll never live it down."

"I'm giving you twenty-four hours. If by this time tomorrow you haven't come clean, I'm spilling the beans." She wagged a finger at him. "And don't think I won't do it, cause I will." But when she saw the look of despair on her colleague's face, she softened. "Look, I know for a fact that

Steven likes you. He likes you very much. So why not give it a chance, mh? You never know what it might turn into."

"Steven likes me?" asked Nicolas, clearly surprised.

"Of course he does. He told me so himself. So you see? There's nothing to be afraid of. And I know it's hard to put yourself out there. To show him how you feel. But I can promise you that you'll feel a lot better once you do." She spread her arms. "After all, what have you got to lose?"

"A lot," Nicolas murmured, but she could see that her pep talk had invigorated him, and had given him something to think about.

"Twenty-four hours," she warned, and left the office. Sometimes she felt she was the actual manager of this place. And maybe she wasn't too far off, either!

CHAPTER 36

Lauren was in her office, checking a customer complaint that had come in online, and trying to make sense of it, when her phone buzzed. She glanced at the device, and was surprised to see that her husband was trying to reach her.

For a moment she considered letting it go to voicemail, but then picked up.

"Jack?" she said, employing her 'busy' voice, hoping he'd make it quick. He'd called her last week, something to do with the twins, and had sounded down for some reason. And since she was trying to get back on her feet, and felt she was doing well, she didn't want to be dragged back into the past—a past where Jack now firmly belonged.

"Hey, Lauren," said Jack. "I just wanted to call and see how you were doing."

"I'm doing fine," she said curtly, as she kept scanning the customer complaint. Something to do with the plumbing, as far as she could determine. So she forwarded it to Cole, figuring he'd want to know. The plumbing in some of the rooms was pretty ancient, and in line for replacement. But as long as the cold war between Grace and Polys continued, there would be no change on that front. And since they were only one-fifth owners now, thanks to Dad, it made no sense investing their own money into the place, only to see it flow straight back into Polys's pocket.

"I was thinking about you," said Jack.

"Is that a fact?" she said coolly. She hadn't thought about him, which had surprised her. After being married for twenty years, she would have expected to miss her husband. But she'd gotten over him remarkably quickly. And in fact now found herself a lot happier and doing a lot better than when they were still together.

"The house sold," he said, sounding sobered now that she wasn't breaking out into rhapsodies, just because he'd bothered to call.

"Yeah, I know. The real estate agent got in touch. Said we got the price we wanted and then some." Which was great, since it meant she would be in a financially much better position again, and could contribute to the cost of living at the house, same as her two sisters.

"I'm back, you know."

"Back where?"

"Back in New York. Well, Glens Falls, actually."

"You moved in with your parents?"

"I did, yeah. Mom had a bad fall, you know, and Dad asked me to move in. He's not so steady on his feet himself, and so living with them I can take care of them both."

"That's nice," she said as she sent the email, and turned to the next one.

"So LA didn't work out so well for me," he said finally, when she didn't ask. "I wasn't selected for the next round of the competition, and so that doesn't seem to be going anywhere." He barked a curt laugh. "They actually said I should probably give up on my dream of being a singer. I lack the necessary talent in that area. Those were their actual words."

She'd always suspected Jack was a lousy singer, which is why it surprised her he wanted to make a career of it. Then again, with enough practice and dedication you probably could pick up any skill. Or at least that had been her thinking. Apparently that wasn't the case. And also, Jack wasn't one for dedication and perseverance. He'd taken up so many hobbies in the past, and dropped them again when they had proven too hard. Like the time he took up carpentry, and wanted to build his own verandah, and a gazebo in the backyard. In the end they had to hire a professional, and Jack had never touched those shiny, expensive tools again. So Lauren had sold them on eBay to recoup some of that money.

"So what are you going to do now?" asked Lauren, only mildly interested, to be honest.

"I don't know. Take care of my folks, I guess. Maybe look for a job in the area."

"As an accountant?"

"Of course as an accountant, Lauren," he said, raising his voice a little. "That's my line of work, after all."

"I know it's your line of work, Jack. But you said you didn't want to do that anymore. That you wanted to follow your dream and quit working for the man."

He was quiet for a moment, then said, "Looks like I don't have a choice, do I?"

"You do have a choice. You've got the money from the house now, so that's something that might launch you along a new path. Maybe work on your singing."

"I guess," he said without much excitement. He sighed. "I miss you, Lauren."

"Mh," she said, noncommittally. Frankly she didn't want to hear what he was going to say next.

"So I was thinking, maybe we should get back together,

you know. I mean, we had a pretty good life, didn't we? We had a great thing going for us. So why don't we forget about the last couple of weeks and pretend as if that never happened."

"But it did happen, Jack. You left me, remember. Because you wanted to start a new life without me. Because I was holding you back from being who you truly are."

"I said a lot of dumb stuff," he said quietly. "And I'm sorry about that. I guess I just felt… trapped or something. Unhappy with myself." He paused. "Maybe I should see a psychologist. Or maybe we could see one together. One of those marriage counselors? Mom tells me Aunt Susie and Uncle Blake are seeing one, and they're very happy with him. They're making some real progress."

Aunt Susie and Uncle Blake had been having marital problems for as long as Lauren could remember, but that was mainly because Uncle Blake was a drunk, and got very nasty when he hit the bottle. No marriage counselor could fix that.

"I don't think so, Jack," she said. "You told me to move on, and so I did." And she had no intention to go back. She hadn't expected it, but she was feeling a lot happier now than when she and Jack were still together.

"I told you to move on because I wanted to move on. But I was wrong. I realize that now. I threw away the best thing I had, Lauren. I threw away what we had. And I see that now. It took some time, but I see that I made a big mistake."

"Look, I'm fine without you, Jack. And I'm sure that in due course you'll see that you're fine without me, too. It's going to take some time, and you're going to have to adjust to your new life, but you'll see that this has all been for the best."

"How can you say that!" he cried, and she could hear he was getting desperate. He clearly was not in a good place.

"What we had was... well, it was just great. And if you can't see that, then... I don't know what to tell you."

"I'm not discounting or diminishing what we had together, Jack. We had twenty years, and some of them were great, and some of them not so much. But you were right. We've changed. You're not the same person you were when we got married, and neither am I. So even though you're having second thoughts now, and even though you took me by surprise, and your decision to leave me was hurtful to me, I think in hindsight it was probably for the best—for both of us."

"Will you please think about it? I... I miss you, Lauren. I miss *us*."

In spite of herself she said, "I'll think about it." But she said it more to end this conversation, which was pointless in her view, than because she was actually going to consider moving back in with her estranged husband. Besides, they'd sold the house, and he was living with his elderly parents now, taking care of them. So she didn't see her moving in with them, too, and leaving Hampton Cove. "Oh, Kitty called," she said. "She and Kimmy want to spend their summer at the resort. Well, here and also at the house, I mean. Is that all right with you?"

"They're not kids anymore, Lauren," he said gruffly. "They don't need my permission, and neither do you." And with these words, he rang off.

She found herself gazing out the window of her office for a moment, thinking about the conversation. Jack's impetuousness had gotten himself in trouble. He'd thrown away his marriage, his career and his home on a whim. Just because he wasn't happy with the way his life was going. And now that things hadn't turned out the way he'd hoped, he wanted to repair the damage. But it was too late for that. She was never going back. Even if it meant spending the rest of her life alone.

Who was she kidding? She'd never be alone. She had her sisters, and she had her mom, and even the resort, whose guests and staff felt like family to her. And of course she had Kitty and Kimmy, the twins, who had been as shocked as she was when Jack left, but who'd rallied wonderfully, and had been a great support to her.

She smiled as she watched Jill standing in front of a small group of devoted guests, putting them through their paces as she taught them some intricate yoga positions. She wondered if Jill would stick around this time. She hoped she would.

CHAPTER 37

Jill had been keeping up a rapid pace, but when she saw how several of her pupils were turning red in the face and were breathing hard, she realized she was being too hard on these people. This wasn't a yoga class in Goa, where her students had been a bunch of young people, well-trained and fit. The average age of her pupils at the resort was upwards of fifty, with the oldest student she had a brave lady of eighty-five, who was remarkably limber for her age.

So she smiled and slowed down the tempo again, and changed tack by selecting easier positions. She wasn't in the business of murdering her class, but of gently nudging them toward a life of greater fitness and health.

She hadn't actually expected to enjoy life at the resort this much. She remembered life at the Hampton Cove as being staid and boring. But that was eighteen years ago. She had changed, and she now realized she actually loved the place. Even sharing a house with her sisters and her mother was a nice change of pace, and not as challenging as she had thought.

All of that didn't mean she would stick around forever, of course. She was a free bird, and might fly the nest at any time. And it was exactly that sense of freedom that made her wonder if she might not stay put this time. She was thirty-six, after all, an age when many start to wonder about the next chapter.

She never had a particularly strong wish to start a family, not like Lauren had at least, but as she spent more and more time at the resort, where a large proportion of the guests were families with kids, she caught herself imagining having a baby. And even though the prospect still scared her, even terrified her to some extent, it also held a certain attraction, and she had to admit it was starting to be within the realm of possibility, which was a big change for her. Major, in fact.

When she told her mom—in the most careful terms possible—about some of these thoughts, Mom had reacted almost ecstatically, and had rattled off a list of eligible bachelors, who would all be most willing and able to fulfill her deepest wish. And so when she told her mom she was thinking about having this baby without the input of a husband or father, Mom had freaked out a little, before calming down, and agreeing with her that times had perhaps changed, and that nowadays a woman could have a baby on her own, and that was all right.

Just the idea that her daughter considered sticking around this time, and not taking off for India or some other part of the Far East, made her mom's eyes sparkle. And so maybe she would do just that. And maybe she would not. Nothing was decided, and all options were on the table. And that's the way she liked it.

She glanced over to the pool, where Grace and Cole Newman were checking some part of the pool drainage system, which was acting up again. They really needed to put in a completely new pool, as this one was old and ready for the scrap heap. She narrowed her eyes as Grace and Cole's heads almost touched. Did they just kiss? It was hard to see from where she was standing.

But just then her oldest pupil asked a question, so she focused on her class again.

* * *

GRACE WAS FEELING AS GIGGLY and girly as a teenager. She and Cole were enjoying a whirlwind romance that had stirred up feelings she'd long ago forgotten existed. They'd gone on a first date, and when that went well, had gone on a second, but pretty soon lost count. They were probably on their fifth now, or their sixth or seventh, but who cared? Things were moving fast—way faster than she had thought possible. Cole had shaved his beard, and had emerged not the ogre she had feared he might have been hiding under all of that facial hair, but a most handsome man. He still resembled the same boy she kissed for the first time twenty-five years ago, but had somehow become even more good-looking with age. He certainly had become a better kisser, but then probably so had she.

They both had plenty of practice, of course, a topic of their third date—or had it been their fourth? When they'd opened up about the boyfriends and girlfriends that had passed in and out of their lives since they'd last seen each other. In Cole's case that was a surprisingly low number. He'd only been with one woman for about ten years, before she had moved on, and so had he. That was ten years ago now, and so he was long overdue another serious relationship.

But they weren't there yet. Though it was certainly starting to feel serious. Her mom also said so. She said all the signs were there. And when Grace had asked what signs, she said she could tell Cole was crazy about her—but then he always was. Even after Grace had left for college, Cole used to ask her dad about her all the time, wanting to know what was going on in her life. After a while he stopped asking, when he realized Grace was never coming back. Which is when he'd started dating his girlfriend, before that also ended.

"So what do you think the problem is?" she asked now.

She had no head for technology, which was ironic, since she'd worked as VP for a tech company for years. But then you didn't need to be a techie to run a tech company, oddly enough. Her MBA had been enough to dazzle Jay Polys.

"The problem is very simple," said Cole. "This thing is old. Too old. And it should have been retired and replaced years ago. The fact that it still keeps chugging away is a testament to your dad and his skill as an engineer."

"You're telling me my dad built this?"

"He did. He didn't like what was on the market at the time, so he put together his own drainage system, and as you can see it has stood the test of time."

"Until now," she said.

"There's a limit to the strains and stresses these things can take, Grace. And this baby right here is screaming to be put out of its misery." When Grace didn't respond, he repeated, "This system needs to be replaced. It's old and broken."

"Like me," said Grace with a sigh. This whole battle with Polys had taken a lot out of her. He was effectively holding them hostage, she felt. He wouldn't invest any money, even though it was clear to anyone that the whole place needed a major overhaul, not just the pool. And to invest their own money seemed pointless, as profits mainly flowed into the pockets of the majority owner.

They were stuck. The resort was crumbling, which drove guests away, and the new owner wasn't lifting a finger, even though he was a millionaire many times over—a billionaire even, according to the business press. Though a portion of that billion he got for the sale of Polys would go to the government, of course, in the form of taxes. Still, it wasn't as if he was stinting for money.

She'd already explained all this to Cole, but even though her boyfriend had a pair of golden hands, he clearly had no head for business. "I don't get it," he said now. "Polys paid your dad for an eighty-percent share of the resort, didn't he?"

"Yes, he did, but Dad had dug a hole so deep that all of that money had to be used to pay off the creditors he owed money to."

"So can't you sell some of your dad's cars or yachts or whatever?"

She patted her chief of maintenance on the cheek. "You poor fish. You don't get it, do you? There are no cars, there is no yacht. It's all gone."

"You're right," said Cole. "I don't get it. How can it be gone?"

"Well, turns out that Dad was an inveterate gambler," said Grace.

It was another family secret she wasn't particularly eager to divulge. But Cole was family—he probably always was—and just about the most discreet person she knew. "He created new holes to fill the old ones. And those cars and that yacht? He never actually bought them. Those were just rumors people spread. So all the money he got from Polys for the sale of the resort? That was to pay back the people he owed—mainly located in Atlantic City, if that rings a bell." This whole gambling business had been news to everyone, and had come as quite a shock to them. It had only surfaced when a gambling buddy of Dad's had attended his funeral, and had spilled the details of Dad's secret life—and addiction.

So Juda hadn't lied when she said Dad hadn't spent all that much on her—he probably spent a lot more on a slew of slot machines and one-armed bandits. He'd been very careful to hide his addiction from his family. None of them had even an inkling. But in the end the truth had come out—even though it was too late.

"So that money is gone?"

"All of it. Gone down the drain of a gambling addiction no one knew Dad had."

"Poor guy," said Cole, causing Grace to look up sharply. "No, I don't mean it like that. I just mean—it's an addiction, isn't it? And it must have been painful for him to be struggling like that."

"It probably was," Grace agreed. Dad should have talked to someone—or they should have paid closer attention to what was going on with him. But the man might not have been a great poker player, judging from his losing streak, but he certainly had a poker face. No one had suspected that he spent his days gambling at a casino instead of running the resort his wife's family had entrusted to him.

"So why isn't Polys investing? Why isn't he doing something about the sorry state of this place?"

"Maybe he hopes you can keep fixing stuff?" she said, partly in jest. "No, I don't know why he's been so reluctant to invest." It probably had something to do with her, though. In fact she knew it did. And the worst part was that he was probably going to sell his stake to some big resort chain, so he could be free of her.

"If he keeps postponing there won't be anything left to fix," Cole said. "No more guests means no more resort. And he'll have wasted his investment."

"Maybe I shouldn't have been so hard on him," she now mused. "Cause if Polys pulls out, his replacement might be a whole lot worse than him."

It was a sobering thought. She disliked Polys, and still resented him for what he did to her, but at least he seemed to have some inkling about what made this place work. If he sold to one of the big players, they'd start from a clean slate: they'd raze it to the ground, and erect one of those lifeless, soulless resorts in its stead. And if that happened, the Hampton Cove would never be the same again.

CHAPTER 38

Bea was enjoying brunch at the resort—a weekly thing that had proven very popular. It was just one of the things she had introduced in her new capacity as PR manager, and one she was particularly proud of. Though she couldn't really take full responsibility, as the idea had been mainly Juda's.

She was sitting with Juda now, and also with Ruth and Jessica, the four friends reunited. They weren't focusing their energy on organizing the flower show anymore, or the other social events they were rightly famous for, but trying to give the Hampton Cove a genuine renaissance, and drive up sales.

"So how are things going with the girls?" asked Juda, while sampling a spoon of the fruit salad she'd ordered. "It must be a big change for all of you, with them living at the house."

"It is," she admitted. The four friends had all ordered different things, and were now sampling them so they could offer a genuine critique to the new chef, who was simply wonderful. He'd joined them from the Argent, which was a nice change of pace, as usually it was the Argent poaching their staff members, not the other way around. She would have liked to think it was a harbinger of things to come, but she knew better than that. The resort was understaffed and underfunded, both things Polys had it in his power to change, but for some reason he couldn't be bothered.

"Are they going to stay, or is this just a temporary thing?" asked Ruth.

"It's a temporary arrangement," she said. "While the girls figure out what they want to do with their lives. We've all been through a lot, you know, and it takes time to get our footing."

"It certainly does," said Jessica, who was the fourth member of the squad. The four women had known each other since high school, when they'd become fast friends, and had stayed close all these years, which was quite an achievement. Johnny had almost managed to end their friendship, but at the end of the day, and after spending a lot of time talking things through, Bea and Juda had made peace with each other. Bea had even come to terms with Johnny's betrayal. When the truth had been revealed about his gambling addiction, it had come both as a great shock to his family, but also as an explanation of how his life had gone off the rails.

"I don't think they'll stay forever," said Bea, "but I have to say I'm very much enjoying their presence. Without them, the house had become so empty—when it was just Johnny and me." A fact which might have precipitated the breakup of their marriage, with Bea burying herself in her work as a local socialite, and Johnny's gambling habit spinning out of control, ending in the sale to Polys.

She actually missed Johnny, now that she wasn't so angry with him anymore. He had been a wonderful husband to her —though these last couple of years they'd shared the house but not their lives—or their hearts. He still had been a great friend to her, and he was always the first one she talked to about anything. That's what she missed most of all: their conversations, and Johnny's friendship.

She had the girls now, of course, but she was realistic enough to know they wouldn't stay at the house forever. At some point Jill would fly off to who knows where, Lauren would return to New York, and Grace would take up her high-powered career again the moment the dust had settled on the big hullabaloo Polys had caused. Still, she had decided to enjoy it while it lasted, and not to pressure her daughters into staying—it just might drive them away sooner.

"Who's that man over there, with Grace?" asked Juda.

"That's Cole Newman. He's in charge of maintenance."

"Of course—Cole Newman," said Ruth. "Didn't he and Grace have a thing way back when?"

"Looks like they're having a thing now," said Jessica.

They all glanced over, and Bea's heart warmed when she saw how well the newfound couple were getting along. "They've been dating again," she said.

"When did that happen?" asked Ruth.

"It's still very new," said Bea. "And I'm not even sure if it will last. But Grace is very happy, and that's all that matters."

"It is, isn't it? The moment you become a mom, it stops being about you, and suddenly it's all about them."

"Until they leave the house," said Jessica. "And then suddenly you find yourself alone again. Quite the adjustment."

"I know," said Bea. Which is why she was so happy right now, hosting her three grown-up daughters.

"Oh, look," said Jessica. "It's that actor—what's his name?"

"Tim Deutch?" said Juda. "I think that's his name."

It was Tim Deutch, enjoying brunch with Olivia Hill, who'd been giving such amazing performances in some of their evening shows. Though Tim wasn't in the kind of movies Bea liked to watch—these blockbuster superhero movies were more for kids, after all—she had seen him in something, though she couldn't remember what. Probably when her granddaughters Kimmy and Kitty were home for the holidays, they'd all watched one of his movies together.

"He's been staying here for a while," said Bea. "I think he's seeing Olivia."

"She's that singer, right?" said Ruth. "She's got such a great voice."

"She has, hasn't she?" said Bea.

"Are they dating, you think?" asked Jessica.

"Judging from the way they can't stop staring at each other, I'd say so," said Ruth. She eyed the couple wistfully for a moment. "I wish my husband still looked at me like that."

"At least your husband is still alive," said Jessica, who was a widow, just like Bea.

"Sometimes I wonder if he is alive," Ruth said, which made them all laugh.

"So what do we think, ladies?" asked Bea. "Points for the chef?"

The consensus was that the chef had outdone himself again, and all of his creations received the maximum score from this expert panel of friends. Another win for the resort, and Grace for having the perspicacity to hire the guy.

* * *

"PEOPLE ARE STARING AT US," said Olivia when Tim pressed a kiss to her lips.

Tim glanced over and smiled. "She's the owner," he said. "Bea Wheeler."

"Oh, that's right. Grace's mom. She's nice." But then they were all nice, of course. All the Wheeler women. It had come as a surprise to her to discover that the resort was actually run by one family, though it might explain the truly delightful atmosphere of the place—one she'd never come across anywhere else.

"I should probably put my disguise back on," said Tim, as he nervously glanced over to two young boys, who seemed to have spotted him, and were whispering furiously, probably getting ready to pounce, their phones in hand for a selfie. "Or soon I'll be spending the rest of the day taking pictures with fans."

"People here really seem to respect you, though," said Olivia. "They're not as pushy as they are in other places."

"No, that's true," said Tim.

It was another one of the differences between the Hampton Cove and other resorts. Here people really seemed to respect a person's privacy, even a person as famous as Tim Deutch. She smiled at the man she still had trouble calling her boyfriend, wondering when she would wake up and discover that it had all been a dream. But there he was, and had been since the night they'd struck up that conversation at the bar, and had gone for a walk on the beach.

Somehow she'd found herself spilling all of her secrets to him, and he had done the same with her. Well, secrets was a big word, but she had told him about the church, and the ordeal they'd put her through. They had both arrived at the resort in the hope of finding some peace and quiet from the events that had rocked their world, perhaps more so in her case than his, and this shared experience seemed to have drawn them closer together from the start.

Their walk on the beach had ended in a tentative first kiss, which had surprised Olivia a great deal. And their relationship had quickly developed from there, going from strength to strength in the short space of time they'd known each other. Tim had proven a gentle, kind and timid man, quite the opposite of his on-screen persona, in fact, which was the brash, adventurous swashbuckling type.

Since then they'd developed a routine: they went for a run every morning, and a swim in the ocean, had breakfast together, once the big crowds were gone, and took trips along the coast, talking about their lives and getting to know each other. And with each passing day, they were growing closer and closer.

It was quite the surprise romance, and she dreaded the day the press would find out, and turn their affair into something tawdry and sordid, the way they always did. Tim had promised her they could stop that from happening, though, and to keep things discreet and out of the limelight. It's what he preferred, actually. He'd had very public romances play out in front of the world media before, and it had never ended well. That kind of pressure was detrimental to a budding relationship. And so he'd vowed not to let that happen again with Olivia.

She had no expectations, though. She simply tried to take things one day at a time, knowing that very soon the world would put its demands on Tim again, and he'd disappear from her life. When that happened, she'd probably be devastated, no matter how hard she tried not to get too attached to him.

But today was one more day they had together—a day she didn't have to share him with the rest of the world. And so she vowed to make the most of it.

CHAPTER 39

Grace was back in her office, poring over the numbers, when there was a soft knock at the door.

"Come in," she said absentmindedly.

When she looked up, the first thing she saw was a gigantic bouquet of white lilies and roses. A smile spread across her face. Fully expecting it to be Cole—who else could it be?—she said, "I see you finally learned to knock. And they say you can't teach an old dog new tricks."

But then the bouquet lowered and instead of Cole's face, it was Polys who emerged.

Immediately her smile was wiped from her lips. But Polys wasn't deterred. "I've never been called an old dog before, but I'll take it as a compliment."

"What are you doing here?" she asked, not in the mood for word games.

"This may surprise you," said her former—and current—boss. "But I've actually come here to apologize." She stared at the man as he took a seat, and set the bouquet on her desk. "These are for you, by the way," he said.

"Thanks, I guess."

"Look, the thing is that I behaved abominably to you. I should never have done what I did, and for that I am deeply sorry." He flicked a speck of dust from his perfectly creased pants. "That being said, I didn't lie when I said I wanted to be involved in the running of the resort. Only I see now that I came off as heavy-handed and maybe even intimidating. I'm used to doing things my own way, and getting what I want, and I realize that when I tried to muscle my way in, I made a mistake. And so for that, too, I apologize. I was wrong, and you were right."

She was too stunned to respond. Jay Polys apologizing to her. Now that was something new.

"Look, I realize we have a history between us, and it's making it hard to work together. So I want to suggest a truce." He gestured to the bouquet. "Hence the color of the flowers. I come in peace, as your humble servant, if you'll have me."

"My humble servant, huh?"

"I've been looking at the numbers, and I have to say you're doing a great job running this place. I should have known you would, since you were the best VP I ever had the pleasure of working with. And so what I would like to suggest is this: you remain in your position as general manager, and I'll stay in my position as the owner, but I'll be as hands-off as you want me to be. I realize that our relationship is fraught with severe difficulties, as a consequence of our shared past, and all I can say is that I hope that in due course you'll be able to forgive me for what I did to you. My behavior was abominable, and I understand that now. I do," he stressed when she gave him a skeptical look. "It was wrong of me. There's no excuse."

"So what about investments? When you came on board you said you wanted to make the necessary investments to turn this place around?"

"And I'm still willing to make those investments. But first we need to decide what the resort should look like in the future."

"*We* should decide?"

"Yes, we. You and me, and the rest of your family. I may be the majority owner, but your family is the co-owner, and it's important for me to recognize that fact."

"What made you change your mind all of a sudden?" she asked, still suspicious of Polys's motives. As a savvy investor, he usually had some trick up his sleeve.

"I want my investment to be profitable," he said with a shrug. "It's as simple as that. And if collaborating with you is the best way to accomplish that, so be it."

"That's a very charitable attitude."

"Look, I recognize the importance of this place to you and to your family, but I'm here now. I bought a big stake, and I'm not going to walk away. So the way I see it is that you're stuck with me, and I'm stuck with you, and so why not try and make the most of it? I think we've got a beautiful project here. People love this place, and have been coming here for decades. It's part of the town's cultural heritage, and a very important part of the fabric of its economic and social life, so let's work together and make sure it continues to be all that into the future."

"Okay, so you're actually going to stick around. You're not going to sell your stake to the Argent, for instance? Or to some big international chain of resorts?"

"No, I'm not," he said. "I've bought a house in town, and I'm here to stay."

Now that was a surprise. "I thought you were going to buy a yacht and become a world citizen," she said.

He smiled. "Obviously you don't know me as well as you think you do. I want to feel like I belong, Grace. I've been getting to know this town—getting to know its people, and I must say I can see the attraction. There's a vibrant community here—not just a bunch of strangers who commute in and out of town and never talk to each other. I can really see myself growing old here—maybe even start a family."

"As long as it's not with me, you're welcome to stay as long as you like."

He laughed. "Thanks. I'm glad you're not going to try and drive me out of town, feathered and tarred."

"You can stay," she said with a smile. "Pretty sure this town is big enough for the both of us."

"So how about you? Are you going to stick around? Or is this just a temporary arrangement?"

She'd been thinking about that a lot, actually. What did she want to do? Did she want to be general manager of her family's resort for the rest of her life? Or try and find some other job? Return to join the big leagues in some capacity if they'd have her? With Jay being as penitent as he was, he might be induced to put his apology into a written statement, published online on some influential business blog or periodical, which would go a long way toward restoring her damaged reputation.

"I'm not sure," she said honestly. "I guess I have to give it some more thought."

"Of course. I just want you to know that as far as I'm concerned, you're the perfect person for the job, and I certainly hope you'll stay on."

"Thanks," she said, warmed by the unexpected praise.

"Now about the future of this place. I've identified several areas that are in urgent need of some much-needed repairs. Could you take a look and tell me what you think? In due course I think we need to go the whole hog and tackle the whole resort. Submit it to a full-scale renovation. The place was built fifty years ago and as far as I can tell there has never been a substantial overhaul."

"No, I guess my grandfather built the resort, and kept expanding over the years, every time he had some money, but there was never a grand vision or a master plan. So the oldest parts of the resort are crumbling."

"Exactly!" he said, sitting up. She could see his excitement exuding from his posture and the expression on his face. Jay Polys was a man who liked to build things. In that sense he had an engineer's mind, just like Dad. And here was an opportunity to build something big—and build it well. "It's almost like a collection of bric-a-brac, a part added here, a wall slapped on there, an extra set of rooms, a tennis court, a nail salon, jacuzzi... There was no central vision—no grand design. So I would suggest we bring in a first-class architect, let him design this place from the ground up, and then we start implementing his ideas and construct the kind of resort we really want to see."

"On one condition," she said.

"Name it."

"That it never loses its family feel. We don't want to construct some cold and impersonal spa resort, Polys. We want to keep the unique atmosphere the Hampton Cove Resort & Spa is rightly famous for. Because if we lose that, we'll also lose our customers—some of whom have been coming here for decades."

"Like Terry and Heather Davis," he said, nodding.

She was surprised to hear him say it. "You know about Terry and Heather?"

"Of course. I may not have shown my face around here these last couple of weeks, but I've kept a close eye on things. I thought that was a wonderful thing you did for the Davises."

"Terry is a great gardener, and Heather has done an amazing job restructuring the housekeeping department. I'd say it's a win for all of us."

"It is, and I hope they'll stay on for as long as they're able to. It's people like the Davises that we need to keep in mind when we redesign this place."

They sized each other up for a moment, and Grace wondered if she could trust this man. She had trusted him once, and he'd stabbed her in the back pretty ruthlessly. Should she risk going through that same experience again? But his apology seemed genuine enough, and so was his enthusiasm to work together, and create something truly remarkable. So finally she nodded. "Okay, let's do this."

A smile spread across his handsome features. He was still sporting the same fashionably trimmed beard, which perhaps was one of the reasons she had become so allergic to beards. "I would like to organize a meeting where we discuss all of this, and come to some kind of formal agreement."

"A meeting? With the architect, you mean?"

"No, with you and your mom and your sisters. I want to do the right thing this time, Grace. I know I screwed up before, and I don't want to do it again."

"Okay, you can have your meeting."

"Great." He got up, buttoning up his suit jacket. "So we have an understanding?"

"We have an understanding," she agreed, and when they shook hands on it, she had a feeling they'd finally buried the hatchet and left this chapter of their lives behind them.

The moment Polys had left, Cole walked in. He must have been waiting. When he spotted the flowers on her desk, his expression darkened. "Trying to win you back, is he?"

"Not exactly," she said.

"So why did he give you flowers?"

"As a peace offering." And she told him about the conversation they'd had. Cole was as surprised as she was, and also visibly relieved, both for the fact that she wasn't thinking about getting back together with her former boyfriend, as for the resort, which just might have a future now.

"Do you trust him?" he asked anxiously.

"I'm not sure. I thought so before, and then he did what he did. So now I'm not sure if he can be trusted. But if we put everything down in a formal agreement, then I guess even he won't be able to wriggle himself out of it."

"I hope so. This place needs some big ideas and a big pile of cash."

"That's one thing Polys does have: he's got some very big ideas, and about a billion dollars to back them up."

She came from behind her desk, and allowed Cole to wrap her in his arms. When they came up for air, she said, "You're still a great kisser, Cole. In fact you've improved."

"I've been practicing," he said, then realized how that sounded, and added, "for you." And when that didn't come out the way he thought, he opened his mouth again, only for her to shut him up with another kiss.

When Steven walked into her office five minutes later, and saw his boss making out with the handyman, he quietly closed the door again, and tiptoed away. "Get a room," he murmured. Though of course technically they had.

CHAPTER 40

Steven entered Hazel's office looking pretty excited. "I've got him now," he announced.

"Got who?" asked Hazel. "What are you talking about?"

"Him! My secret admirer."

"Oh, God. Is that still a thing? I thought that was all over by now."

"It's not over. He sent me another message this morning. Only this time I've got him!"

"You're speaking in riddles, my young friend. Please explain."

"I hung a camera in the lobby, aimed at my desk. And when I look at this footage," he said, waving a USB stick, "I will finally know the identity of the man who's been sending me these messages."

"You haven't looked yet?" asked Hazel, who seemed interested.

"No, I wanted you to be there when I looked." He handed her the USB stick. "Here. You look first, and then when you think it's safe for me to look, I will."

"What are you talking about? Let's look at the thing together."

"I will not!" he said, stomping his foot. "What if it's someone I know? Oh, the tension is simply too great! I can't take it, Hazel—I just can't take it anymore!"

"All right, all right," said Hazel. "Here, I'll preview it for you, and then I'll tell you what's going on, okay?"

"Just do it," said Steven, chewing on his fist as he eyed the booker nervously. He squeezed his eyes closed.

"Stop fidgeting already," said Hazel.

"Are you watching it?" asked Steven.

"I'm watching it."

"Can you see who it is?"

"I'm amazed by the clarity."

"You should be able to scroll through quickly. It's equipped with a motion detector, and I turned it on after I left last night, so not many people should have entered the lobby, except our resident poet—my mystery admirer."

"Oh, will you look at that?" said Hazel.

"What?! What is it!"

"A duck walked into the lobby. And then walked out again."

"Oh, Hazel, please don't joke," he said plaintively. "This is no time for jokes!"

"I'm not joking. An actual duck walked into the lobby. Must have been looking for a room."

Steven opened his eyes again, and saw that Hazel was regarding him with a look of amusement on her wrinkly face. "It's fine," she assured him. "You can look now."

"Who is it?" he whispered, shoving his other fist into his mouth and assaulting his knuckles with his teeth.

"Come over here and have a look. Go on—take a look. It's all right."

But when he stubbornly shook his head, his heart

hammering in his chest, she simply turned her screen, and he suddenly found himself looking into the face of… Nicolas!

"But… that's Nicolas," he said. "Where is my mystery man?"

"I think Nicolas *is* your mystery man, Steven."

"But… but how? Why? What's he doing?" he asked, studying the accountant's movements. First he put something on Steven's desk, surreptitiously looking around as he did, and then suddenly he approached the camera, looked straight into the lens, and mouthed, 'I love you, Steven,' and formed a heart with his fingers!

"He says he loves me!" Steven cried, tears springing to his eyes. He fluttered a hand to his face. "How did he know about the camera? I didn't tell anyone."

"Nicolas is no fool, Steven. He must have realized you put it there."

"He loves me," said Steven, swallowing once or twice. "Which is convenient, as I love him!"

Suddenly the door swung open, and Nicolas burst into the room. The two men eyed each other for a moment, both prey to powerful emotions, then clasped each other into their arms, and as Hazel rolled her eyes, the romance was all too perceptible.

HAZEL MAY HAVE ROLLED her eyes, but she was actually glad to see these two young hearts finally coming together. It had taken them long enough! After she'd told Nicolas to get his act together and to confess to Steven that he was his secret admirer, she was fully prepared to tell Steven herself when Nicolas hadn't made a move when his time was up.

But the accountant had pleaded with her to give him more time, and had promised he'd declare his love for his colleague in the right way and at the right time. He wanted to do something grand—something memorable. Though Hazel thought he was simply not ready yet. So she promised not to say anything until he was.

So when she had seen Steven hanging up his camera in the lobby, she told Nicolas, who had finally overcome his trepidation, and had made his big gesture.

"And now if you could take this stuff somewhere else," she said gruffly, and ushered the young couple out of her office. She didn't mind public displays of affection, but not in her place of work!

At least everything was well that ended well. And now hopefully there would be no more of those dreadful poems. Though knowing Steven and Nicolas, she had a feeling this new romance might be fraught with some potentially interesting challenges. Life at the Hampton Cove was never boring!

Polys was in the lobby, texting on his phone, when he unwittingly became a witness to a most unusual phenomenon: the young man at the reception desk, one Steven Lesinske if his information was correct, and it was, had emerged from one of the offices in the administrative wing, clutching the hand of that young accountant Nicolas Holmes. And as they burst into the lobby, suddenly they kissed.

The tech billionaire's jaw dropped at the surprising spectacle, and when Grace Wheeler came upon the scene, she clocked the couple, noticed Polys's expression, and said, "In the last place I worked a thing like this wasn't condoned. In fact a person I know was fired for kissing her boss."

Polys nodded. "I guess her boss was a jerk."

"He was, though he has since apologized."

"And did you accept his apology?"

"I did. I think we turned a corner. Don't you?"

She was eyeing him closely, he saw, and had never looked more beautiful. "I would say so. And I'm glad that we did." He took a step closer. "Could I induce you to have dinner with me? We could work some more on turning that corner."

But that big, burly handyman had now also popped up out of nowhere, and he was giving Polys a not-so-friendly look. So Polys took a step back again. He watched as the handyman took Grace by the shoulder, dipped her down, and planted a big kiss on her lips. He straightened her again, and Grace, looking distinctly flustered, said, "I guess that's a big no on that dinner, boss."

Polys grinned. Message received loud and clear. And as he walked out of the lobby of the resort he co-owned, he thought that the place was inhabited by crazy people. But lucky for him they were exactly the right kind of crazy people. His kind, in fact. And if he'd ever been in doubt whether sticking around was the right thing to do, there was no doubt in his mind now. He was definitely here to stay.

CHAPTER 41

A year had passed since Grace and her sisters had taken over at the helm of the Hampton Cove Resort & Spa. It had been a turbulent year, both for the three sisters personally, and also for the family business, which had been on the verge of going under. But luckily a turnaround had been achieved, even though Jay Polys revealing himself as the investor Johnny Wheeler had brought on board had looked ominous for a while.

Polys had settled in and had become quite a fixture in Hampton Cove social life. As was his habit, he had begun putting his mark on things, and there was even rumor that he might run for mayor at some point, though whenever asked, he firmly denied the rumor. He was dating a local now, a woman who ran the local art gallery, and the couple were clearly happy, as Polys had already been introduced to her family, and she to his. It was a strange turn of events for the tech billionaire, though not stranger than the trajectory his life and career had taken, and continued to take.

Bea Wheeler watched as Polys seated himself next to his girlfriend, a plate in his hands, and thought the man had come a long way. The spring festival she was organizing at the resort was a resounding success, not just with Polys attending, but with almost all of the townsfolk, and many guests. The resort was finally on firm financial footing again, and the renovation was well underway. After Grace and Polys had made peace, the family had approved the plans for a comprehensive renovation effort. They hadn't closed down the resort, though, instead opting to spread the work out over a longer period of time, and gradually working through a long list of smaller campaigns, giving guests a reduced rate while the renovation was going on—compensating for the nuisance and the noise.

Many people didn't mind staying at a resort that was under construction, though. Some of them even loved it—they eagerly followed the work in progress, and took pictures with the workers. For kids especially it was instructive, to see how a construction site operated. They had to stay behind safety barriers, of course, and did.

Bea glanced around at her three daughters. They were still living at the house, but she had the impression they might not stay there for very much longer. Jill had a boyfriend now, a man she met while teaching yoga. He was also a yoga teacher, and worked at the Argent. He'd heard about her class, and had been curious to see a colleague at work. He must have liked what he saw, for he asked her out that same day. They were thinking about moving into an apartment in town, which meant that she wouldn't skip off to India again—thank God!

Grace was sitting with Cole, chatting animatedly as usual. The couple had been inseparable, but even though Cole owned his own studio apartment, it was too small for the two of them, and also, Grace was pregnant, so they were looking for a place of their own—preferably as close to Grace's childhood home as possible.

And then there was Lauren, whose divorce had come through a couple of months ago. She and Jack were going their separate ways, and as far as Bea was concerned, that was a good thing. She'd never liked Jack very much, and after what he did to Lauren, she had liked him even less. For now Lauren was still staying at the house, along with the twins. Kimmy and Kitty were home from college, and having the time of their lives. And so the house was filled with love and laughter, and more family than Bea ever thought would fit in. But they were making it work, and she loved every minute of it.

She saw how Lauren was talking to the architect who'd done such an amazing job redesigning the resort. Saul Burk had taken the old resort, and incorporated it into his plans for the new one. And in so doing, skillfully combined the old and the new, with the utmost respect for what was, but also with an eye to the future.

Bea had noticed that Lauren and Saul were spending a great deal of time together, and judging from the way he was looking at her, it was obvious that the spark of love had touched the man's heart. She wished them well, as Saul seemed more suited to Lauren than Jack had ever been. And the great part was that Kitty and Kimmy had also taken a liking to him. Saul was divorced, with two boys the twins' age, and Bea saw that the four teenagers stood chatting together, and seemed to enjoy each other's company as much as their parents enjoyed theirs.

The great thing was that Saul owned a house in town—in fact very close to Bea's. A person can only dream, but it was her fondest wish that all three of her daughters would choose to stay closer to home this time around. And who knows? It just might happen. She'd gone through so much this past year, that she felt she was in line for some happiness.

Who were also looking distinctly happy were that young

movie star Tim Deutch and his new wife Olivia Hill. The couple had married in the fall, and their union was soon to be blessed with a baby. Bea had a long conversation with Olivia, who had become part of a local band called Due Course, and was a fixture at the resort. Olivia said that Tim had broken all ties with his agent, and was now with a new agent, who respected his wish to act in movies both big and small, and to alternate between the kinds of small productions he loved, while also appearing in the blockbuster fare that was so popular with the kids these days.

After the wedding, Tim and Olivia had bought a house, just down the road from Bea. So they were neighbors now, and Olivia had already asked Bea to be her designated babysitter—if she wanted to. Of course she had said yes, and being around so many young people made her feel young again herself, and invigorated.

All in all it had been quite the year for her—and for her family. But they'd taken on the challenges life had thrown in their path, and grown from the experience. In fact her life now looked better than it had before.

"This is such a wonderful festival," said Heather Davis, who was seated next to Bea.

"It is, isn't it? I couldn't have done it alone, though." Her friends Juda, Ruth and Jessica deserved most of the credit, as they'd taken on the big job of organizing the resort's events calendar with the same dedication they took on their social calendar. "How is Terry, by the way? Isn't he coming?"

"Oh, but he's here," said Heather, who'd been running their housekeeping department like a well-oiled machine, and had proven herself a most valuable addition to the team, just like her husband. And now Bea saw that Terry stood talking to Polys, waving his arms as he did. "Terry's got a new project," said Heather proudly. "He wants to turn the roofs of the resort into rooftop gardens. Says it's a win-win on all accounts: it's going to cool down the rooms located underneath, lowering the resort's AC bill. And guests can go up there and enjoy the scenery. It's going to be grand. He's got some very good ideas."

"Looks like he's found himself an eager listener in Polys," said Bea. The investor stood nodding fervently, as he listened intently to Terry's pitch.

"I like Polys," said Heather. "I didn't like him at first, but I like him now. I think he's changed."

"I think we've all changed," said Bea. Though she didn't know why, something had happened to change all of their lives. Not just her daughters, but also Terry and Heather, Steven and Nicolas, who were a couple now, Hazel Heflin, who was more or less the heart of the resort, and the person everyone confided in, Terry and Heather, of course. But also Polys, and even some of the guests.

"It's this place," said Heather. "Your dad wanted to create a safe haven for families—a place where you can feel at home, and where you can make friends. It's a unique thing in this world of ours, you know, a place like this."

"A family place," said Bea.

Heather smiled. "You know, Terry and I weren't blessed with a family, but coming here year after year, we never seemed to mind so much. And now that your daughter was so nice to give us a permanent home in one of the bungalows on the premises..." She paused, overcome with emotion as she thought back to those dark days a year ago.

Bea rubbed her back. "It's all right, Heather. You're all right."

"We found our family, you know," said Heather. "You're our family."

"I know. So maybe that's the secret. My dad built this place for his family, and in the process turned everyone who visits into one great extended family." And to think she hadn't wanted to bother with the resort for so many years. Imagine what she had missed. At least she had been lucky enough to find it again. And then her daughters had stepped in and had saved the place. Though Johnny also had a part in that. True, her husband had lost his way, but in the end he'd done the right thing by bringing Polys on board—who had been instrumental in bringing about a true renaissance, creating a place for future generations.

Heather clinked her glass to hers, and then her daughters joined them, and they all toasted to a bright future—for the resort, and for their extended family. And to Bea's dad, who was looking down on them—hopefully with pride.

And as Bea got up to check on the catering, a man sidled up to her, and gave her an engaging smile. His name was Jacqui Barnes, and he'd been a close friend of her husband.

"Wonderful party," he said. "In fact I can't remember having enjoyed the spring festival as much as this year."

"That's because we didn't have one last year, or the year before," she said.

"That might be the reason I don't remember attending last year's edition," he said with a smile. He eyed her closely. "You look well, Bea. You had us all worried there for a moment, after what happened to Johnny, but you seem to have snapped back from those terrible events."

"I have," she said, well pleased that Jacqui had noticed. She didn't know him all that well, but remembered always seeing him hovering in the background for the many years they'd known each other. He was a widower, just like her, and had lost his wife about a month before she had lost her husband. "And how about you, Jacqui? How are you holding up?" she asked, realizing she probably should have asked him this question a year ago. But then her life had been in such a turmoil for such a long time she hadn't been particularly involved in other people's lives. But all that had changed. The stronger she was starting to feel, the more involved she became in her local community once again.

"I'm fine," said Jacqui, who was about her own age. "Bella had been sick for a while, so her passing didn't come as a great surprise. Still a big shock, of course, but we had a long time to prepare ourselves for what was to come. Though one keeps hoping for a miracle."

She nodded, and noticed for the first time the kindness of the man's eyes. They were entirely focused on her right now, which provided her with a little frisson of pleasure, she had to admit. "Johnny always spoke very fondly of you, and of Bella."

"He was a good friend. Perhaps not such a good husband, but a good friend."

"He was a good husband—only he lost his way at some point."

"Yeah, if only he'd talked about it, we might have been able to help him. But that was Johnny. He liked to play his cards close to his chest. He was a proud man, and didn't want his problems to be known to anyone. That's just how he was."

They were both quiet for a moment, remembering the man Bea had married, and spent the greater part of her life with. The memories had ceased to be bitter, and now more and more the good ones were drifting to the surface, of which there were many. They'd had a good life together, and raised three wonderful daughters.

"Could I..." Jacqui began, and she noticed he was suddenly looking slightly nervous. "Could I perhaps—if you're not too busy, of course—take you out to dinner one of these days, Bea? Nothing special—just two old friends having a nice dinner and a chat."

She smiled. "Of course. I'd be happy to have dinner with you, Jacqui."

His smile was something to behold. A mixture of relief

and pleasant surprise, it suddenly made him look ten years younger. He was actually very handsome, she saw. "I've never told you this, Bea, but I've always had a great admiration for you."

He eyed her fervently, then shyly looked away. So she slipped her arm into his, and together they walked in the direction of the drinks table, chatting amiably and catching up on old times. It may have been the atmosphere of the party, or the springtime, but suddenly she had the impression that romance was in the air.

THE END

Thanks for reading! If you want to know when a new Nicole Saint book comes out, sign up for Nicole's mailing list: nicolesaint.com/news

ABOUT NICOLE

Nicole Saint has a background in political science and before being struck by the writing bug worked odd jobs around the world (including but not limited to massage therapist in Mexico, gardener in Italy, restaurant manager in India, and Berlitz teacher in Belgium).

When she's not writing she enjoys curling up with a good book, Netflixing romcoms, Christmas-themed Hallmark movies, rewatching The Holiday for the hundredth time, sampling pastry, perusing comic books, twisting herself into a pretzel by doing yoga, and spoiling her big red tomcat Tommy.

www.nicolesaint.com

OTHER TITLES

The Princess

The Resort

Hampton Cove

CPSIA information can be obtained
at www.ICGtesting.com
Printed in the USA
LVHW031743200423
744807LV00011B/574